HAMLET
DREAMS

Jennifer Barlow

Durham, North Carolina

Library of Congress Control Number: 2001118204

ISBN 0-9706225-1-1

Cover art by Frank Wu

Cover design by Sang Lee

Aardwolf Press
P.O. Box 14792
Durham, NC 27709-4792
www.aardwolfpress.com

For Dan, the prince who kissed me awake.

Author's Acknowledgments

I would like to thank, for their help and inspiration over the years: Guy Hail, a Clarion West classmate who was there when this story was no more than a gleam in my mind's eye; Sibyl, who helped me find the courage to keep trying; my mom, who has always believed in me; and Al Bellak, my dad, without whom this book would not have been possible.

Thou mayst not wander in that labyrinth;
There Minotaurs and ugly treasons lurk.

—*William Shakespeare*

1

On a miserable late-summer day when the North Carolina sky had been inclined to burst into violent thunderstorms at the slightest provocation, Zac pulled his VW into the gravel parking lot that fronted his building, and cut off the windshield wipers and then the engine. He stepped out—into a mud puddle—and slogged toward his apartment, holding last Tuesday's newspaper over his head, a feeble umbrella that quickly disintegrated in the wind-whipped rain. His shoes oozed muddy water with every step; he pried them off outside his door and left them on the landing—it wasn't as if someone were going to steal them.

Inside the small apartment, Zac peeled off his wet clothes, took a long, hot shower, and pulled on his battered terry cloth robe. It was nearly six, and Cecile wouldn't arrive until eight; that gave him two hours to get the place clean.

Better get started, he thought.

But as he surveyed the kitchen sink, overflowing with dirty dishes; the living room couch, littered with junk mail and newspapers he hadn't yet read; the carpet, dotted with dog hair that had come home with him from work; he knew he didn't have the energy. He needed to unwind first.

He needed to be in the Other Place.

Sprawling on the sofa, he rested his head against the cushions and propped his feet on an empty pizza box. He closed his eyes, breathed deeply through his nose, and let his mind wander. Over the years, he had been to medieval fortresses atop cloud-covered hills, to dank stone corridors lit by blazing torches, to lazy Mediterranean villas. He had spent days in Lilliput, nights in Avalon, mornings in Sherwood Forest, and evenings in the Hall of the Mountain King.

Today, Zac wasn't in the mood for adventure. He wanted to go where it hadn't rained in years and where there wasn't a barking dog within fifty miles. Maybe a deserted tropical island, where he could sit on the beach and watch the waves while the sun-warmed sand soothed his tired muscles.

He relaxed his jaw, his fingers, his mind, until he could almost hear the cries of the seagulls and the roar of the ocean. It reminded him of the Outer Banks, last month, him and Cecile. They would have to go back there in autumn, he thought. People had told him that the beaches were deserted in autumn. He couldn't imagine anything more romantic than to be alone on a beach with Cecile.

Reluctantly, Zac opened his eyes. Thinking about Cecile was one of his favorite pastimes, but it seemed to make passage to the Other Place impossible. To get there, his thoughts had to drift, not focus.

He dragged himself off of the couch and trudged into the kitchen, where he loaded and turned on the dishwasher. Its roar filled the apartment and made his head hurt—it sounded too much like the constant din of the hair dryers at work—so he retreated to his bedroom and closed the door.

Folding the load of clean laundry he'd dumped on a chair two days ago, Zac felt his headache worsening. He rubbed the bridge of his nose where the pain gathered, and swallowed two aspirin tablets, dry. Then he flopped onto his bed and buried his face in a down pillow that had once belonged to his grandmother . . .

. . . and found himself sitting on a wide stone step, his calves twitching as if he'd just finished a brisk jog.

Wiping sweaty palms on his jeans, he shook his head. He was in the Other Place—that much was clear. But how? A delayed reaction from his earlier attempt to get here? He stood up, confused and disturbed.

The step he'd been sitting on was in the middle of a long flight that stretched up a hill, beyond his range of vision. The stairs were enormous—each about six feet in width—and were bordered by large rocks painted in red with the flowing script of a language unknown to Zac. A river of people marched up and down those stairs, many of them dressed in red and gold robes.

Squatting beside Zac was a skinny boy, maybe eight or ten years old, his head covered in a thin fuzz of black hair, as if it had been shaved recently. The boy scrambled to his feet and took firm hold of Zac's hand. "You want see temple, Joe?" He smiled eagerly and tugged at Zac's hand. "Come. See temple." He led Zac upward.

The stairs were not steep; even so it took Zac about two and a half paces to get across each one, making for an awkward climb, full of stops and starts. Soon, his legs were throbbing and he indicated to the boy that he wanted to catch his breath.

The boy seemed anxious to continue, but Zac rested and watched the activity around him. A troop of monkeys surged across the stairs, chattering, scanning the hands of the people moving past, probably hoping some of those hands held food they might steal. An old woman, who had been nibbling a piece of bread, clutched it closer to herself when a monkey suddenly lunged for it. Zac's young guide scooped up a handful of pebbles and flung them, like buckshot, drawing screams of protest from the animals, who scattered and were soon gone.

Speaking rapidly—but no longer in English—the boy tugged at Zac's hand, and they resumed the climb. Farther on they saw other monkeys, or maybe it was the same troop spiraling up the hill. Once, a troop fled headlong down the stairs, shrieking and calling to each other. Several of them had scarlet cuts on their bodies. Zac decided they must have been in a fight, perhaps with another troop whose territory they'd invaded.

Still the boy pulled Zac upward. The broad stairs gave way to a much steeper flight, and Zac looked up and groaned. His legs ached with fatigue and his heart pounded. He wanted another rest before tackling this next obstacle.

Stopping for breath, he looked back, and his eyes fixed on a monk, approaching from behind. The man was bent almost double, and clutched a thick walking stick in hands gnarled with age. His face was a mass of wrinkles; Zac thought he must be at least seventy-five years old. The monk did not even pause before the steeper stairs, but continued climbing at his methodical pace.

Zac had never thought of himself as one of those "out-of-shape Americans"—he did, after all, lift, wash, and brush dogs all day for a living—but now he wondered. Gritting his teeth, he started up the stairs again, the boy nodding his approval enthusiastically.

A few more minutes of climbing, and Zac began to feel dizzy. Was the altitude, the effort, showing on him? He breathed deeply, bringing more oxygen into his body, but the dizziness redoubled, and he staggered.

The boy propped him up. "Not now, Joe," he said. His face was fearful and he pulled urgently on Zac's arm.

Zac took another unsteady step, clinging to the boy.

"There! There, Joe!" the boy cried.

Higher up the hill, at the base of what had to be the temple, a monk with shaved head and red and gold robes was throwing rocks at the monkeys. Not the pebbles the boy had thrown to scare them; these rocks were large and aimed to kill or maim. The monkeys howled and bared their teeth, standing their ground against the monk's rage. The old monk Zac had noticed earlier had halted his steady progress to gape at the conflict, a horrified expression marking his ancient face.

A rock hit one of the monkeys and sent it rolling limply down the stairs, almost to Zac's feet. Where the rock had struck its head, a bloody line parted the monkey's fur.

The boy tugged on Zac's arm one more time. "Bad man! You help!"

Zac tried to step forward. The dizziness halted him, and he suddenly remembered that his exit from the Other Place invariably followed a spell of dizziness. He looked up once more. The monk had ceased throwing rocks and was staring down at Zac through greedy, eager eyes, his lips contorted into a hateful snarl.

The sky tilted, like a plane banking sharply . . .

. . . and Zac was lying on his bed, a hand shaking his shoulder. "Zac, are you all right? Please wake up!" The voice had a frantic edge to it.

He opened his eyes to find Cecile bent over him. Her face was white, and she sighed with relief when she saw that he was awake.

"You scared me!" she said, putting her hand over her heart and taking a deep breath. "I couldn't get you to wake up!"

Rubbing his eyes, shaking his head to clear the cobwebs, Zac mustered a smile for Cecile. "I'm sorry," he said. "I was dreaming. I must have been really tired." He rubbed his eyes again and glanced at the clock beside him. It was 8:15. "I didn't mean to fall asleep, so I didn't set the alarm."

Cecile smoothed his hair. "That's all right. Are you sure you're okay?"

"Yeah," Zac said, but even so, he wondered. Normally, he snapped right out of what he called his "Hamlet dreams," whenever his phone rang or the alarm went off, sometimes even when an ambulance siren wailed nearby.

Nothing about this one had been normal, though. He still remembered that monk with his feral eyes and that snarling mouth. Suppressing a shudder, he stretched, swinging his legs over the edge of the bed.

Cecile sat down beside him. She had gotten a haircut since the last time he'd seen her. The difference wasn't striking, but she no longer had the frizz of split ends. Zac put his hand to her soft brown hair and ran his fingers through the strands all the way down to her shoulders. "I like it," he said.

"You noticed!" She smiled. "Bess and I had a bet over whether you would or not."

And surely it had been Bess who'd bet I wouldn't, Zac thought. What Cecile's roommate had against him he didn't know; maybe it was that he hadn't been instantly attracted to her, as most men were.

"So, what do you want to do tonight?" he asked. He could hear the rain pounding relentlessly on the roof, accompanied by the howling wind and the rumble of distant thunder.

Cecile moved to sit closer to him. "I don't think we should be going out in this weather," she whispered, her lips brushing his cheek. "Do you?"

Surprised, Zac turned his head to receive her kiss. He put his arms around her and pulled her closer. Her hands caressed his back and her breasts pressed against his chest. But when their lips parted, her gaze was fixed shyly downward.

Tentatively, Zac reached for the top button of Cecile's blouse. Her customary refusal wasn't forthcoming; instead, she was pulling on the belt of his robe. He kissed the top of her head, all he could reach as he struggled clumsily with her buttons.

Pulling her shirttail from her skirt, Cecile took over the unbuttoning of the blouse. Zac gently raised her chin with his fingers, to meet her eyes. On Cecile's face was an expression he could not read. It didn't look like passion, though Zac supposed he wasn't the best judge of that. It didn't look like nervousness either, though he was sure that was what she would see on his face.

He kissed her again, his hands pushing her blouse off her shoulders, then traveling over the smooth, bare skin of her back until they found the hooks of her bra. Her skin prickled with goose bumps as Zac pulled the bra over her shoulders and tossed it on the floor, then ran his hands lightly over her body. She burst into giggles and accidentally bit his lip.

"Sorry," she said. "That tickles."

Caught between amusement and annoyance, Zac held her more firmly and pressed her down onto the bed, lying on top of her, careful not to crush her with his full weight. He kissed her lips as his hand slid up her skirt toward her panties.

Cecile went rigid beneath him. He felt the sudden tension, felt it all through her body, though she still returned his kiss.

It was one of the hardest things he had ever done, but he rolled off of her. She had come so close!

"Are you all right, sweetheart?" he asked, stroking her hair. She closed her eyes and he saw a glimmer of moisture in her lashes as she turned from him.

"I'm so sorry," she said miserably. "I just can't." She cried quietly, and Zac stroked her neck in silence.

"It's all right, Cecile," he said when he could finally trust his voice. "You know I'm willing to wait."

She sat up, scrubbing at her swollen eyes. "I had made up my mind that tonight would be the night. I was . . . so sure that . . . " Her voice trailed off, but Zac didn't interrupt her. "I want you to know that it's not you," she said. She put her soft hand against his cheek.

He took her hand and kissed it. "Is there some way I can make it easier for you? Maybe I'm being too pushy, or—"

"No, it has nothing to do with you. Please believe me."

"Then can you tell me what's wrong?" he asked.

Cecile shivered and shook her head. "Not tonight," she said, her voice barely a whisper.

"Did somebody hurt you?"

Her eyes widened and she shook her head violently. "Please don't ask me any more questions." She was about to cry again, and Zac knew he'd found the answer. He pulled her into his arms and held her tightly.

Cecile softly pushed open the door of her apartment, but Pantagruel foiled her effort at a silent entry. The chocolate poodle barked and ran about the apartment, his claws making tiny ripping sounds at each turn.

The light under Bess's door came on.

"Oh, Panta," Cecile whispered, "you're not supposed to bark at *me*, stupid."

Bess pushed open her bedroom door and leaned bleary-eyed against the frame. She stretched hugely, her short night-gown creeping upward to show more and more of her thighs. Her short, auburn hair was tousled and she wore no makeup, but she exuded a casual sensuality, even at this hour, that Cecile admired and even envied.

"So, how'd it go?" Bess asked. "I'd say from the expression on your face that either it went badly or it didn't go at all."

Cecile wished mightily that she hadn't confided in Bess. After the long heart-to-heart they'd had yesterday, and all of Bess's well-intentioned advice, how could Cecile admit that she'd spent the entire night *sleeping* in Zac's arms?

She dropped her purse on the dining room table and plopped herself down on the couch. She wasn't up to this, not now. Now, she wanted only to pretend that last night had never happened.

She saw Bess's bare feet walk past her into the kitchen, then heard the running water. Soon the telltale aroma of brewing coffee filled the apartment. Bess always made it strong—stronger than Cecile liked—and then added extra sugar, as if that would make up for it.

Returning to the living room, Bess handed Cecile a steaming mug and sat beside her on the couch. "Okay, kiddo, tell me what happened."

Cecile sighed. "Nothing happened. Not a thing. I just couldn't do it, Bess." For a moment she thought she was going to cry. She blinked quickly and took a sip of the too-strong, too-sweet coffee.

Bess put a hand on her shoulder. "To tell you the truth, honey, I never thought you would."

"What do you mean?"

"Don't take this wrong, Cecile, but remember, I have met this boyfriend of yours. He's not exactly the kind of man a woman loses her virginity to."

Cecile's cheeks warmed. "That's not what you said yesterday." Yesterday, when Bess had urged her not to wait for the perfect romantic moment, to just do it and get it over with.

Bess shrugged. "It was worth a shot. And you'd have felt like shit if you hadn't tried."

"And how would that be different from how I feel now?" Cecile regretted the sullen words as soon as she'd spoken.

"The fact is, Cecile, if you're scared about doing it the first time, then the last person you need to be with is some virgin who's probably as scared as you are."

"You're wrong, Bess. I love Zac, and he's good for me. He's patient, and—"

"A little less patience and a little more skill would—"

"Why do you always have to see him in a negative light?"

Bess finished her coffee and set the mug down on an end table. "I know you feel you love him and all," she said, "but you have a problem to work out, and he's not helping you any."

Cecile shivered and hugged herself.

"I know you have nightmares," Bess continued. "And after what you told me yesterday, it's easy enough to guess they're about Steve. You're not going to like this, but I have to wonder if you're going out with Zac just because he's as different from your stepfather as anyone you've ever met and you think somehow that makes him safe."

Cecile stood up abruptly and carried her coffee into the kitchen, spilling out the cooling remains into the sink. "I appreciate what you're trying to do, Bess," she called from the kitchen. "But that's going too far. This conversation is over."

Bess followed her into the kitchen. "Sorry. I'm not trying to hurt you."

Cecile wondered if that were really true. Bess wasn't above hurting her "for her own good."

"Too bad things didn't work out between you and Jerry," Bess said pensively.

"You don't quit, do you?" Cecile put her coffee mug into the dishwasher and slammed it shut.

"Of course not!" Bess smiled. "When have you ever known me to quit, roomie?"

"Could you *try* to make an exception? Just this once?"

"All right. For you, anything. But if you decide you want to talk later . . . "

"Thanks," Cecile said, though at that moment she felt more like slapping her smug face than thanking her. How much longer would she be bringing up wonderful and sexy Jerry? Cecile had asked Bess once why *she* didn't pursue him if she thought he was such a god. Bess had merely shrugged and said something about the chemistry not being there.

"Well, I'd better start getting ready for work," Bess said, and she left the kitchen.

Cecile put her head in her hands and told herself one last time that she was not going to cry about this anymore.

Zac looked at his watch. It was after nine o'clock. Cecile wasn't going to call tonight.

He had known how upset she was Saturday morning, though she had tried hard to hide it. He had let her leave, knowing she wanted to be alone. But she hadn't called him since, and tomorrow was the first day of classes at Sarah Walden, the exclusive girls' school where she taught. She would have no time for him during her first week of classes, and there was so much they had left unsaid.

There was a knock on the door. Zac sat up, his heart pounding. Cecile had never come over without calling first; then again, Cecile had never spent the night in Zac's bed before, either.

He opened the door. "George?" he said, realizing only after the word had left his mouth that he sounded like an idiot.

George's mouth quirked. "No, his evil twin. May I come in?"

Zac opened the door a little wider, allowing his older brother to enter.

"This place smells like dogs," George remarked.

"Nice to see you, too. If you'd let me know you were coming I'd have had it fumigated and sterilized. Anyway, I don't know how you can smell anything through all that Old Spice." Zac had often wondered what George's patients thought of a psychiatrist who smelled like perfumed stationery.

"Sorry, George. Ignore me. Here, have a seat." Zac moved a pile of newspapers off of one side of the couch for George, then sat down in his favorite chair. "So, what brings you out this way?" George seldom came to Zac's apartment. He considered the neighborhood a slum, said he was afraid to walk there. The neighborhood didn't bother Zac, but he supposed if he wore a Rolex like his brother, he might worry more.

George eyed the sofa with evident disdain, then sat down gingerly, as if afraid something might bite him. "Dad wanted me to come talk to you."

"Not again," Zac groaned.

"Just listen, will you? There's an opening at Dad's firm for a clerk. It's a good job, Zac, and you're perfectly qualified for it. Why don't you at least give it a try?"

"Maybe I don't want to be a law clerk. Has that thought ever occurred to you?"

"It pays a hell of a lot more than washing dogs."

"Dad made sure of that, no doubt."

"What did you go to college for if you're planning to groom dogs all your life? Mom and Dad made a lot of sacrifices to put you through school."

"Save it. I've heard this speech from Dad enough times. I don't see them suffering from the drain I put on the family."

"That isn't the point. The point is you've let them down."

"They've got you, Mr. Brilliant, what do they need me for?" Zac heard the jealousy and anger in his own voice and wished he'd kept it to himself.

"Is that what this is about? Listen, I've worked hard for what I have, and if you worked half as hard you could make something of yourself. Go to graduate school, if you don't want to be a clerk. If you were moving forward, you know Dad would help you out financially."

"George, I've had it with school, and I don't want some boring desk job. Maybe someday I *will* decide this isn't for me and I'll go back to school and become a doctor just like you and I'll have my own practice and a beautiful wife, a three bedroom house and a Mercedes. But for now, I just want to be Zac the dog groomer."

George shot up from his seat as if he were about to storm out of the room, then took a deep breath and sat back down. "Do you ever listen to yourself talk?" he asked.

"What do you mean?" Zac said.

"This jealousy business has got to stop." Zac opened his mouth to object, but George shook his head. "Don't bother. I can accept that you don't like me. But you're still family, and I refuse to be the one holding you back."

"George, much as you would like to think so, my life does not revolve around you or any jealousy I may or may not feel."

"Why do *you* think you're an underachiever, then?"

"Because I don't put the same emphasis on money and status that you do, I guess."

"Is it that, or are you afraid? Afraid to try, and maybe fail?"

"Hey, I'm not one of your patients."

George shook his head. "I knew it was pointless to try to talk any sense into you." He stood up, and this time he stayed up. Zac barely made it to his feet before George had reached the door. "Give me a call if you change your mind," George said, and he pulled the door shut behind him.

Muscles taut, Zac returned to his chair, picked up a book, and flipped blindly through its pages. There was nothing wrong with the way he lived. He had grown up surrounded by nice things, in a nice neighborhood, with nice parents who had nice jobs. That hadn't made him any happier. The kids at school had still picked on him, the girls had still shunned him. Now that he was old enough to control his own life, he would live it the way he chose. He made enough money to pay the rent.

After reading the same page three times without absorbing it, Zac threw the book down on the coffee table, causing a minor avalanche. He didn't care. He visualized the same books and papers and trash tumbling down in the center of George's immaculate living room, and smiled brightly.

At bedtime Zac took an antihistamine, knowing it would make him drowsy. Maybe he could get to sleep without worrying about Cecile or stewing over George's insinuations. He set his alarm, then stretched and slid into his bed, suddenly so tired he didn't need to wait for the drug's effects. He settled on his right side . . .

. . . and someone grabbed his wrist in a powerful grip, twisting his arm painfully behind his back. An olive-skinned giant with a black beard was binding Zac's wrists together with coarse rope, its individual threads cutting into his skin as the rope tightened.

He was surrounded by a dozen men, soldiers. His torn tunic lay on the ground to his left and the rays of the sun heated every inch of his naked body. One of the men shouted in a language Zac didn't recognize. Another pulled a bronze dagger from his belt and held the point against Zac's ribs. When Zac didn't respond, the two of them seized his arms and dragged him forward, and Zac realized that they wanted him to walk.

"All right, all right," he said. His speech surprised his captors. They looked to one another, suspiciously, angrily, fearfully by turns. Finally the leader motioned sharply, and the troop of soldiers began walking, shoving Zac along before them.

Thirty or forty minutes they marched, through a landscape so barren that all Zac saw were flat fields of dying, brown grass. Then, far ahead, he made out a stone wall, fifteen or twenty feet high, gently curving, stretching as far as the eye could see on both sides. The soldiers were leading Zac along a path where the brown grass had been trampled to dust, a path that led to the only gate in the wall.

Wherever this great wall was, it was no place that Zac had ever visited before, and he thought he should be excited and eager to begin this new adventure; instead the setting left him uneasy, and a voice within him repeatedly murmured that something was very wrong.

As he neared the wall, Zac heard a clattering sound, as if somewhere a chain were winding around a spool, and the gate began to swing open, its hinges squealing loudly. One soldier untied Zac's hands, and another shoved him through the opening; then quickly the gate swung closed, and the men turned and marched away at a brisk pace that to Zac's mind spoke of fear.

Inside the great wall stood another wall, no less high or imposing, though at irregular intervals along its length there were rectangular openings. The two walls were so close together that Zac could put one hand on each without raising his elbows from his sides. He glanced left and right, but both directions looked about the same.

He had just decided, for no particular reason, to explore to his right, when he heard a soft hiss behind him. He whirled around.

On the other side of the gate's iron bars, a figure, draped in a dark cloak and hood, beckoned to him. Zac moved closer and peered into the shadowed hood, searching for a face, but could discern only the glitter of eyes.

The figure laughed and shook off the hood, revealing a mane of curly red hair. Her skin was pale, with a spot of rosy color on each cheek, and her eyes were so dark Zac couldn't see her pupils. A golden circlet rested across her brow, and her thin lips curled into something between a smile and a grin.

Her coloring—Scandinavian pale—and her twentieth century makeup proclaimed her to be as much a native of this world as Zac was. "Well, are you going to speak to me," she said, "or are you just going to stand there with your mouth hanging open?"

Zac flushed, fighting the urge to cover himself with his hands as this strange woman stared. "What is this place?" he asked.

The woman laughed, a deep, throaty sound of genuine amusement. "You don't know? Are you an amnesiac, or has fear addled your brain?"

He continued to squirm under her gaze. She was like no one he had ever met in the Other Place. "Who are you?" he asked her.

"You may call me Ariadne."

He recognized the name from Greek mythology. Ariadne, daughter of Minos. "So that would make this the Labyrinth of Crete?"

She nodded. "Very good. Perhaps now that you have your bearings you are ready to receive my gift." She reached into the folds of her cloak, allowing Zac just a glimpse of bare white skin beneath. He glanced away, but from her chuckle he knew she was aware of the effect that one glimpse had had on him. Whoever she was, she was beautiful enough to render Zac awkward as a randy teenager. What he wouldn't give to have that tunic back!

"That wasn't the gift I had in mind," Ariadne said, "but you can dream." From beneath the cloak she pulled a sword, a little longer than Zac's arm, and passed it hilt-first through the bars of the gate. "I think you may find it easier to kill the Minotaur with this than with your bare hands."

He took the sword. It was light enough to be a toy. "You're supposed to give me a ball of twine so I can find my way back."

"I know the legend," she said.

Zac looked up sharply. "The real Ariadne wouldn't speak of this as a legend."

"I said you could *call* me Ariadne, not that I *was* Ariadne. In the myth we're lovers, but you don't remember me making love to you, do you?"

"Will you?" he asked with a bravado he didn't feel.

"And let you abandon me on some island? I think not." Her eyes examined every inch of his body, enjoying the arousal he could not hide. She put a hand over her mouth, as if to conceal her mocking smile. "The Minotaur at the heart of the labyrinth is no myth. It was released from its cage the moment the gates closed. It has had plenty of practice finding its way through the maze. You don't look strong enough to beat it to death barehanded. Would you rather I gave you a ball of twine?"

He glared at her.

"I can't open this gate," she said, "so finding your way back here wouldn't help you anyway."

"Is there another way out of this maze, then?"

"Killing the Minotaur is the best way. But then, you can always try to wake up."

The blood drained from his face. "You know this is a dream?"

Ariadne shook out her hair and laughed at his distress. "Yes, my dear Hamlet. I know you dream. And I know your fears. 'For what dreams may come when we have shuffled off this mortal coil must give us pause.'"

Zac grabbed the bars of the gate with sweat-slicked hands. He recognized those lines. "Hamlet was speaking of death," he said, ashamed to hear a quaver in his voice. "Are you?"

Ariadne smiled and blew him a kiss. Then she raised her hood once more and turned from him without another word.

Zac stifled the impulse to shout after her. Whoever and whatever she was, she was no friend of his, and anything else she might say would be suspect.

For the first time ever, Zac tried to leave the Other Place before some real-world influence called him back. He closed his eyes and concentrated on the feel of the mattress against his back. He imagined himself lying in his bed, his blanket clutched under his chin, the overly warm comforter bunched up at the foot of his bed, heating his feet and calves until they sweated.

Nothing. The reality was that he was standing with his naked back against a cold stone wall.

With a heavy sigh, he started toward the first opening of the labyrinth. Perhaps he could salvage an adventure out of this unexpected trip, before his alarm clock woke him. After all, how many people had actually matched wits with the Labyrinth of Crete?

Knowing that the way to solve most labyrinths was to keep turning in the same direction, Zac entered the first opening and turned to his right. Gray stone pressed in on him from all sides—walls so close together that sometimes he scraped his knuckles against them when he swung his arms.

The cobblestone floor, too, seemed at times to rise beneath his feet, surrounding him in a cave of gray. Even the weeds that grew up between the stones of the floor had long ago died and lost all color.

After only five minutes, he had to stop and stare up into the sky to assure himself that he was not being smothered. The inner walls were as high as the outer ones, and seemed to lean in upon themselves so that Zac could see only a thin strip of blue sky, a strip that seemed to grow thinner with time. Were the walls closing in on him? The sensation became so powerful that he had to walk with one hand against each wall, to assure himself that they stayed in place.

At many of the intersections of corridors, Zac saw marks on the wall, marks that looked to have been scratched by a human hand. He knew that many captives before him had tried to solve this labyrinth. Had any of them escaped? In the myth, he remembered, only one man had survived: Theseus. Am I Theseus, he wondered?

Time stretched, and the sky above slowly darkened as again and again Zac found himself trapped in dead-end passageways, each exactly the same. His frustration with these dead ends eventually faded into apathy. He had no reason to believe that his escape depended on solving the labyrinth. No, the only way out of here was through waking up. And he was beginning to wonder if he ever would.

The "right turn rule" was doing him no good; Zac abandoned it, now turning whichever way his confused sense of direction suggested. If only the walls weren't so tall, if only they weren't so close together, perhaps I could enjoy this puzzle, he thought. Instead, he wanted only to get his head outside the walls, to where the air moved and the fading sun could touch his skin. He glanced up at the darkening sky. And knew he should try to reach it.

Leaning his back firmly against one of the walls, he walked his feet up the opposite wall. It took most of his strength, but he held himself there, suspended over the stone floor. Pressing hard with his arms and feet, he inched his torso up the wall a bit, then his right foot, then his left. The cold stone bit into his flesh, scraping his back raw as Zac slowly struggled upward, his muscles trembling with the effort. If he could just reach the top, he would see the entire labyrinth laid out before him. Perhaps he could move along the top of the walls. If not, he could at least map out an escape route.

Higher he pushed, until the ground was far beneath him. Knowing he must be near the top, he twisted his neck just enough to look upward, and his eyes met with a sight that made his heart sink.

The top of the wall was set with small metal spikes, needle-sharp, so many that there would be no place for a handhold. Whoever had designed the labyrinth had recognized this avenue of escape and had fortified against it.

Zac's knees weakened and buckled, until he could no longer brace himself. Plummeting to the stone floor, he landed hard on his left shoulder, knocked the side of his head solidly against the wall, and lost consciousness.

2

The Sarah Walden School for Girls had been a stylish hotel in the 1800s, and an even more stylish boarding school at the turn of the century. It looked nothing like the antiseptic public schools Cecile had visited when first looking for a job, schools with cookie-cutter buildings and institutional tile floors. Here, the floors were made of wood. Every summer the wood was refinished, and on the first day of school the floors gleamed, and the faint smell of wood polish permeated the halls and classrooms.

As Cecile walked up the main staircase, she ran her hand along the banister and noticed how it, too, gleamed. It occurred to her suddenly that she loved this school, loved its turn-of-the-century atmosphere, its tradition, its wood. There was a sense of history to the place, a sense of past grandeur that kept her coming back every year.

In her three years at Sarah Walden, Cecile had established a comfortable routine for herself, and it was easy, even on this first day, to fall into it. First, down to the teachers' lounge to put her books and her lunch bag in her cubby. Then a mug of the execrable school coffee that, even at 7:30 in the morning, tasted like it had been sitting on the warmer for three hours. Finally, up the main staircase toward the secretary's office to check the bulletin board for messages.

Cecile was thinking how silly it was to check for messages this early on the first day of school, when she saw the yellow note with her name on it. She pulled it off the board and replaced the thumbtack.

Cecile: I have not forgotten you.

The note was written in an unfamiliar hand—not the secretary's. Frowning, she flipped the paper over; there was nothing on the back. She ducked into the office.

Clare Weiss, usually the only other person here at this hour of the morning, was at her desk looking bored. She smiled when she saw Cecile. "Still getting here at the crack of dawn?" Clare asked. "I would have thought you'd be tired of that by now. I know I am."

"Force of habit, I guess." Cecile replied, smiling. How many times would she have this conversation with Clare as the years went by? "By the way, I was wondering if you saw who put this note on the board for me?"

Clare glanced at the note, then shrugged. "Sorry, no. It wasn't there when I came in, and I haven't seen anyone else this morning. No one else gets here this early, except maybe Chuckles."

Cecile winced. "Chuckles" was what some of the students called Mrs. Stanhope, Walden's headmistress, when they thought no one could hear. It was dangerous enough for them, but Clare was risking her job, using the nickname in public. "If you really hate working here, keep calling her that," Cecile said.

"Relax. She's not around right now. She and Princess Rose are having breakfast in the Residence. I don't think you have to look any further than that for your correspondent."

Cecile nodded, but she knew it was not Rose Stanhope who had written this note. The handwriting was not hers, and even if she had gotten someone else to write it, the message was too subtle for Rose.

I have not forgotten you. What was it about those words that set Cecile's nerves so on edge? There was a hint of menace to them somehow.

She stuffed the note into her pocket, wondering why Clare hadn't seen who'd put it on the board. Clare's desk faced the doorway, and even if she'd been busy, she would have heard the creaking of the floorboards.

Cecile's own footsteps set off that creaking now as she made her way toward the rear staircase that led back down to the teachers' lounge. The door to the stairway squealed as she pushed it open, and when she stepped onto the tile landing, she noticed an extra squeak of the floorboards. Startled, she turned to look behind her. The corridor was empty, and the building seemed abandoned, with its still-dark classrooms.

She swallowed hard. She had not imagined that sound. "Who's there?" she called quietly.

A few yards down the corridor, a narrow hallway branched off, leading to the janitor's closet. There was no light in that hallway—the janitor would not arrive until much later. Cecile heard another creak. She paused, holding the door open, shivering. This is ridiculous, she thought. That note was an infantile prank, and no one is lurking down that hallway.

All she had to do was walk over and look around the corner to dispel her fears. She took a deep breath, and stepped forward, until she could barely peer down the hall. It was too dark to see to the end, but she *could* see the light switch, a few steps into the hallway.

She slid her foot forward, until one toe barely penetrated the darkness; but she could not will herself to go farther. Her heart pounding, she backed away from the hall, and hurried toward the stairs, and as she pulled open the stairwell door, she glanced backward. Nothing had sprung out of the darkness to chase after her; the corridor was empty. She started down the stairs, trying to laugh at her foolishness, but finding that she could not.

Cecile made her way to the teachers' lounge, poured herself a second cup of coffee, and sat in a stiff wing chair beside a dim lamp. The lounge was in the school's basement, and though there was one high window, the new gym that had been made possible by a generous donation from one of Walden's wealthiest alumnae blocked out any daylight that tried to creep into the room.

Across from Cecile's favorite wing chair was a dark, gloomy painting of the original Residence—the heart of the old hotel. After the hotel had been converted to a boarding school, the Schoolhouse had been built, and the Residence had become a dormitory for the girls. Now, its top floors held apartments for teachers and their families, while the lower floors housed the dining hall, the auditorium, and a few classrooms devoted to music and art. Newer, more modern buildings now dominated the campus, but the Residence remained the grand symbol of the Walden School, all other buildings tied to it through a web of tunnels and corridors.

From one of these tunnels now, Cecile heard the echo of footsteps. Her hands spasmed on the arms of the chair. The footsteps were definitely masculine—heavy and sure, the soles of the shoes making a firm thud. The heavy tread sounded angry, storming down the hallway like . . .

Cecile shook her head violently. What was the matter with her? She released her death grip on the arms of the chair and took a long, deep breath. But as the footsteps came closer, her fists clenched tightly again, until she felt her nails biting into her palms, and when Jerry Garret finally turned the corner and stepped into the room, she let out such a loud sigh of relief that he raised an eyebrow at her.

He smiled in the familiar, quirky fashion that Bess found so appealing. How he managed to look so sexy wearing a plaid jacket with leather elbow patches and round wire-rimmed glasses Cecile had never figured out. Perhaps it was the contrast between the outer trappings of an ultraconservative English teacher and the mischievous sparkle of his eyes. Perhaps it had to do with his pierced ear (though she had never seen him wearing an earring), which hinted at a different lifestyle altogether when he was away from school. Or perhaps he was just the male version of Bess, exuding sensuality at any time of day.

"Who were you expecting," Jerry asked, "the ghost of your father?"

Her face went white, and she stood up abruptly. "What?"

Jerry laughed. "You know, Hamlet. People seeing the ghost of Hamlet's father haunting the castle walls."

She noticed, then, the worn paperback copy of *Hamlet* that was tucked under Jerry's arm. Of course. It was the standard beginning for his senior English class. Cecile laughed with him, but the sound came out hollow and nervous.

"What did you think I meant?" Jerry asked.

"Nothing. I just . . . Never mind." The warmth of her cheeks told her she was blushing, and Jerry's expression told her he noticed. He stepped a little closer, his arm raised as though he meant to put his hand on her shoulder, but he stopped just short.

Cecile appreciated his restraint. That she had broken off with him last year after only a few dates had not curbed his enthusiasm, and she had been dreading his renewed attentions all summer long. He had phoned her a few times in July, but she hadn't been home. Bess had taken messages, but Cecile had not called back. She felt a little guilty about that now as he looked at her with such concern.

"Are you all right?" he asked. "You don't look well."

"I'm fine," she replied, forcing a smile. She sat back down and fished in her bag for a book to read—anything to keep Jerry at a distance—but before she could find one, he was already talking to her.

"Why do you keep running away from me, Cecile?"

She let her bag drop back to the floor. "We're at school, Jerry. Can we keep our conversation on a professional level?"

Jerry sat down in the chair across from her, and looked around the room. "It seems to me that we're alone and we can talk about whatever we want."

"Maybe we don't want to talk about the same things."

He sighed. "Maybe not. But we still have to work together, and if you keep running away from me like a scared rabbit people will talk."

"If you'd stop chasing me, I wouldn't have to run," she snapped, with more heat than she usually allowed herself.

"Well, now, that's what I wanted to talk to you about. That's why I got here so early today—so I'd have a chance to smooth things over with you before school starts and things get all awkward again. You never returned my phone calls this summer."

Cecile ignored the reproach, focusing on the fact that he had come to school early specifically to see her. "Did you leave a note for me on the bulletin board?"

He looked puzzled. "A note? No. Why?"

She shook her head. "I just got an odd note on the board and I don't know who left it." She almost bit down on her tongue. The last thing she wanted to do was draw Jerry into a discussion of the vague sense of dread that had plagued her since she had pulled that note from the board. "I'm sorry I never called you back," she said. "I had a lot on my mind."

"I suppose you thought I was chasing you again. I can't blame you for that, I guess. But I was actually calling to tell you I'd gotten married."

Cecile looked up sharply. "Married?!" She noticed for the first time the gold band on his left hand.

Jerry laughed. "Is it so amazing to think that a woman might want to marry me?"

Cecile shook her head. "No, it's . . . just so sudden."

He shrugged. "Well, Kate had been married before, so she wasn't up for the big white wedding thing. Doesn't take long to plan a justice of the peace wedding. And when you meet the right person, taking the plunge is easy." He stood up. "Anyway, I just wanted you to know that I'll be behaving myself from now on." He smiled at her once more. "I hope that means we can be friends."

"Of course. Congratulations, Jerry. I'm sure you'll be very happy together."

Jerry practically glowed. "We already are. See you at lunch!" He flashed her one last smile from the doorway.

Cecile was left feeling strangely empty. In her mind's eye, she saw the girls in Jerry's English classes, gazing at him with adoring eyes. She knew they talked about him in the locker room and in the hallways between classes, and any one of them would probably swoon if he so much as smiled at her. What would any of those girls, even the prettiest of them, not have done to have been in Cecile's shoes while Jerry was pursuing her? Being wanted by a man like that, even when she didn't want him back, had felt good.

Already praying for this day to end, she picked up her bag and trudged off to her first class.

Zac tried to convince himself that the throbbing in his temples was a mild headache, that he was finally waking from this dream. Then he felt the stone slabs beneath his palms, and fear gripped his heart. What if he couldn't go back?

He'd been out a good while, for night had descended, and only the faint light of the moon illuminated the narrow passages. He staggered to his feet, groaning, and started walking. Each step reverberated through his aching head, and the blood pounded in his temples.

Deep from within the darkness behind him, ever so softly, came the echo of a footfall. He turned and strained his eyes in the direction of the sound, but saw nothing.

It happened every time he rested. A phantom footstep, or the sound of a pebble skittering across the stone slabs. He walked faster, so fast that he had to pause finally to catch his breath; yet when he stopped, the sound was closer.

"Leave me alone!" he shouted into the darkness, his voice cracking with fear. He held Ariadne's blade out in front of him, his hands shaking. For a moment, all was silent and still. Then came the sound of footsteps once more—this time not muffled by distance—and a deep, rumbling snort.

The struggle to remain calm was lost, and Zac turned and fled, tripping over loose flagstones, careening into walls, until he ran himself into a dead end, nearly knocking himself senseless. His breathing came in loud, ragged gasps, and he put his hand over his mouth to smother the sound.

The footsteps were fast approaching, accompanied by animal-like snorts and grunts. Zac peered into the darkness, his back pressed hard against the wall, both hands tightly clutching the sword.

A feeble beam of moonlight penetrated the clouds, and Zac saw within it a shadow, huge and broad, darker than the darkness around it, moving toward him. The dim light reflected off an eye, an eye narrowed with hate. The Minotaur stepped into view.

It didn't have the bull's head Zac had expected. Its head was a ferocious, snarling snout of shaggy hair and sharp teeth that looked like it had been ripped off a wolverine and jammed onto the body of a woman at the shoulders. At the join, a bloody red line was visible beneath the thinning fur. The woman's body had perhaps been beautiful once, but now her skin was yellowed and flaking, spotted with bulbous growths.

The creature dropped to all fours—an awkward position for its human body. It lowered its head to the ground, sniffing. Then, it began crawling toward Zac.

He dropped the sword and screamed out loud, screamed, and at once was hit with such an overwhelming surge of dizziness that he fell to his knees. The world twisted and turned around him . . .

. . . and he reached for his shrilling alarm clock and held it close to him as if it were his lost love. When he was finally able to let it go, he read its dial. It had been ringing for ten minutes.

Cecile glanced at the clock on the wall. The second hand seemed to be moving in slow motion. She finished writing the list of vocabulary words on the blackboard and turned to face her French IV class once more.

Rose sat in the back row, her chair tilted backward on its hind legs. When she had first come in, she had tried to hide the gum she was chewing, but now she chewed with open mouth. She met Cecile's eyes with an impudent smile. Any moment now she would blow and pop a bubble, and the other girls would expect Cecile to discipline her.

"Are there any questions?" Cecile asked the class, her eyes avoiding Rose. The second hand continued its slow but inexorable course. No one had any questions. Five minutes till lunch time. Mrs. Stanhope hated it when a class was let out even a minute early. Rose's cheeks were puffing out to blow her bubble. "Class dismissed," Cecile said hastily.

Rose grinned at her just to let her know she was aware of the effect she was having. She blew her bubble and popped it noisily just before slipping out the door.

When the last student had left the classroom, Cecile sat down heavily on her chair. What on earth was she going to do about Rose? Cecile had dared, last year, to give Rose a detention for coming to school out of uniform, and had been forced to endure Mrs. Stanhope's lengthy lecture on how difficult it was for poor Rose to function at a school where her mother was headmistress, and on how Cecile was being less than benevolent for publicly humiliating the girl. Cecile had meekly apologized, then fled to the bathroom and cried, out of repressed anger and frustration. As far as she was concerned, Rose Stanhope's only major fault was having been raised by a mother unable—or unwilling—to see any of her child's flaws.

Now that the girl had learned she could break the rules with impunity, she would be impossible to manage, and the other girls would be jealous of her privileges. Cecile's only consolation was knowing that next year Rose would be safely installed at some unlucky college. And that Mrs. Stanhope had no other daughters.

She supposed she could have a conference with Mrs. Stanhope, seeking her advice. As long as Cecile came as a supplicant rather than a combatant, surely Mrs. Stanhope wouldn't take offense. It wouldn't do any good, though. If Mrs. Stanhope had any idea how to discipline her daughter, Rose would not be the problem-child she was.

Stress had stolen Cecile's appetite, and her head was beginning to ache, so she didn't join her fellow faculty members at their table in the cafeteria. Instead she returned to the teachers' lounge, closed the door, and looked up Zac's work number in the Yellow Pages. He probably couldn't talk to her much from work, but even a moment might reassure her that he wasn't angry with her, that he wanted to see her again. It would be one less worry to plague her through this day.

She dialed the number, regretting that she had waited this long. He deserved an explanation for Friday night; she just hadn't been ready to tell him about her stepfather, Steve. Even now, nine years later, she still had nightmares, the night was still vivid in her memory.

He had stormed down the hall and exploded through her locked bedroom door, the smell of Scotch strong on his breath, fury glowing in his eyes. It didn't matter to him that Cecile's mother hadn't wanted to hear about his girlfriend, hadn't believed Cecile. He had promised retribution should Cecile ever reveal what she knew.

The punches she had expected. Reeling from the pain, clinging to her dresser to keep upright, she had urged herself to grit her teeth and bear it. When her mother saw the bruises, she would finally see the truth about Steve, how full of rage he was, only barely controlled, and how the alcohol set that rage free.

A beating was a small price to pay to get rid of him, and Cecile knew that her mother would divorce him after this. But as she lay curled into a protective ball on the floor, the blows stopped coming, and when she finally risked lifting her head, she saw Steve pulling on the fly of his jeans.

When her mother walked in, Steve had Cecile pinned face down on the bed, her clothes torn and her face bloody. She had kicked and fought and bitten and scratched. In the end, that and her mother's early arrival had saved her, though in reality she never truly felt saved. Did it matter that Steve had never managed to penetrate her? Was she any less violated?

The courts had thought so. Cecile could never forgive them for that. Steve was out of jail before she finished high school. A slap on the wrist, and he was a free man.

"Pet Parlor," a woman's voice answered, practically shouting over a roaring sound in the background that Cecile knew came from the hair dryers that Zac always complained about.

"May I speak to Zac, please?" she said.

"I'm sorry. Zac's out sick today. May I help you?"

"No. Thank you." Cecile put down the phone. She started to dial Zac at home, but thought better of it. If he was sick, he might be sleeping.

She smiled to herself. This was her chance to make it up to him. She would stop after work at the Chinese take-out restaurant they both liked, and bring him dinner. It was a perfect peace offering.

Her stomach rumbled. Maybe she was hungry after all.

There was one little flaw in Cecile's plan, she realized as she pulled into the parking lot of Zac's apartment building, the scent of soy sauce emanating from the brown paper bag on the passenger seat. It was only 4:30.

She could have gone home and waited until dinner time to pick up the food and drive over, but Bess would have noticed instantly that she was upset and would have prodded and pried until Cecile told her everything about this day, from the finding of the note, to Rose's impudence, to Jerry's surprising marriage.

Cecile parked her car and crossed to Zac's door. There was no answer when she knocked, but she could hear movement inside.

"Zac?" she called. The peephole in the door darkened; then the door quickly swung open.

"Cecile!" Zac exclaimed. "Come in. I thought it might be my brother coming back to resume yesterday's argument."

He opened the door wider and she stepped in. He looked terrible, his hair standing on end, his eyes sunken. He obviously hadn't shaved, and he was still wearing the torn, faded shorts and t-shirt he called his "pajamas."

"How are you feeling?" Cecile asked.

He looked at her blankly.

"I tried to call you at work. When they said you were out sick—"

"Oh, right. I just couldn't face going to work today." He noticed for the first time the bag in Cecile's hands, and sniffed the air. "What have you got there?"

"Chinese take out. I thought since you were supposedly sick . . . "

Zac smiled, the pallor melting from his face. "You brought me dinner. Thanks." He took the bag from her hands and kissed her lightly, tentatively, on the lips. Her heart ached at the uncertainty of his kiss.

"I guess it was really just an excuse to talk to you," she said.

He had started toward the kitchen with the bag, but stopped in his tracks and turned to face her. "Since when have you needed an excuse?"

"I thought after Friday . . . "

Zac dropped the food on the kitchen counter then came back to her and put his arms around her, holding her so tightly against his chest she could hear his heartbeat. "Cecile," he whispered in her ear, "nothing you can possibly do or not do will make me love you any less."

Those were just the words she wanted to hear, and she wrapped her arms around him, squeezing as hard as she could. Bess was wrong. Zac was the one for her, the *only* one for her, and he would wait for her and one day she would be ready.

When Zac finally released her, she reached up to touch the stubble on his cheek. "So, if you're not sick, what's really wrong?"

He looked away and shook his head. "It's pretty complicated. I just . . . I didn't sleep well last night."

"Is that your way of saying you don't want to talk about it?"

He sighed. "I guess so," he mumbled. "Forgive me. The whole thing is so bizarre, and I don't even want to think about it. I've been thinking about it all day, and you can see what good it's done me."

She realized she didn't want to talk about her own day either. "Let's forget about it, then. It's nice out. We can go to the Gardens and just forget this day ever happened."

Zac's eyes lit up with the idea. "What about dinner?" he asked, nodding toward the kitchen.

"I'll put it in the fridge and we'll nuke it when we get back. You, meanwhile, are going to change your clothes and do something about that hair."

Zac put his hand behind her head and kissed her, his stubble scraping her cheek. There was no uncertainty in his kiss this time, and Cecile's heart raced as the weight of the day's troubles fell from her.

There were a good many people in the Gardens on this mild late-summer day, though many of them were strolling toward the gates, starting home for dinner. Zac slid his arm around Cecile's waist as they walked down the gravel path between two perfectly manicured beds of petunias toward the wisteria-covered gazebo. The sweet-smelling wisteria flowers were long gone now, but the deep green leaves still draped artfully down the roof, a few tendrils dangling over the side and fluttering in the breeze.

Cecile leaned her head against Zac's shoulder as they stepped into the gazebo and took in the panoramic view of flowers that spread on each side of the staircase. Slowly they walked down those stairs, their arms around each other. At the bottom, they followed the winding path to an open, grassy, field. All around were people throwing frisbees or footballs, tanning, reading on blankets. At the other end of the field, two boys were tormenting a panting dog that exuberantly pursued their frisbee as they tossed it back and forth. Every time the dog would stop, looking comically perplexed, one of the boys would beckon to it with the frisbee and, tail wagging, it would surge forward only to have the frisbee sail over its head once more. Zac laughed, and Cecile joined in with him.

"Let's sit awhile," she suggested, pointing to a shady spot under the spreading branches of a magnolia tree.

"You'll ruin your skirt."

"I don't care," she told him, and she laughed. This morning she had wondered if she would ever feel carefree again.

So they sat beneath the tree, arms still locked about each other's waists, watching the game of catch until the two boys tired of it and gave up the frisbee to the delighted dog. Zac rubbed his chin against the top of Cecile's head. She closed her eyes and leaned into him a little harder. Then, he was kissing the top of her head. Slowly, she looked up at him. His lips never left her, kissing her forehead, her eyes, her cheek and finally her lips. His mouth still tasted of mint from his mouthwash, and his skin smelled faintly of soap. Cecile breathed deep of him. She felt the tentative touch of his tongue in her mouth, and her pulse soared. This was how it was supposed to feel! It was happening! It was finally happening!

When Zac pulled away, breathing hard, Cecile reached for him. "Don't stop!"

"If I don't stop now, I don't know how I ever will!" he said, and blushed.

Cecile supposed he was afraid she would take offense at that. "I guess I know now what you felt like Friday night," she said ruefully.

He met her eyes, looking for some hint of reproach; when he saw none, he broke into a boyish grin. "I guess you do at that."

He put his hand to her hair and stroked it, and she smiled at him. Her fears had receded into Zac's kiss, and in those few moments, she had glimpsed the possibilities of the future. Did Zac have any inkling of the breakthrough he had just made?

She lay down in the grass and looked up at the sky, and he lay beside her, his side touching hers. "You don't know what you've meant to me, Zac," she said. "You make me feel good in a way I never have before." Her pulse had calmed, but the memory of the passion remained with her. It had been wrong of her to deny him the explanation he deserved. Painful though it was to talk about the past, about Steve, she knew she had to, and this seemed the perfect moment. "You were right, on Friday, you know. Someone did hurt me." She fell silent for a moment, then said, "I'm sorry I couldn't tell you about it then. I was scared. Scared that I'd never be able to forget. Now I think maybe I might."

Zac said nothing. He didn't even squeeze her hand, which was the least she could have expected.

"Zac?" She sat up. He lay beside her, his eyes closed. Asleep. "Zac, wake up!" she said. She shook his shoulder, hard. Her pulse was racing once more, but now from fear.

She shook him again, with all her might. "Wake up!" she shouted. People noticed her mounting hysteria; she sensed them gathering around as she shook him and shook him.

Zac whirled around, his eyes barely absorbing what they saw: a dark, deserted hallway lined with statues and paintings, each highlighted with a single spotlight; a marble floor, red as a raw, bloody steak; a high, domed ceiling with incongruous wooden rafters. He didn't have to look too closely to know that somehow, impossibly, he had traveled to the Other Place. While he was wide awake. While he was with Cecile.

What must she be thinking?

He had almost managed to convince himself that last night's horror in the labyrinth had been caused by the antihistamine. He *had* taken aspirin before the strange temple dream. But today he had taken nothing. He had not tried to come here—in fact, he ardently wished he had never discovered the place.

He shivered, in part from fear, in part from the biting cold of the hallway. He chafed his arms. His bare feet quickly grew numb from the chill of the floor.

Gradually, the light brightened until he could see that the hall was very long—so long that he couldn't see to either end. He took an indecisive step forward. A statue gleamed in the spotlight directly in front of him: the Venus de Milo.

Or was it? Zac frowned. What was it about the statue that didn't seem quite right? He looked carefully at the cold, beautiful face. She was smiling! The real Venus was not. As he watched, the smile broadened, so slowly he might not have noticed, save that the smile drew her lips away from her teeth, and the teeth slowly parted.

Inside the statue's mouth, something moved. Zac's feet were rooted to the floor as he stared. The mouth opened in a great yawn, and from inside came the glow of a pair of eyes. With a loud hiss, a snake, black and impossibly fat, oozed its way out of the statue's mouth, its forked tongue flickering, its obsidian eyes fixed on Zac. He finally found the will to move.

A premonition of danger made him turn and look above him. On the ceiling was a panel from Michelangelo's Sistine Chapel, the masterpiece of God creating Adam. Only, God's fingertip was not extended to Adam; it was pointing at Zac. God's eyes glowed red and His lips were twisted into a snarl that showed sharp fangs. The hand peeled away from the ceiling, reaching toward Zac with thick, dark claws. Zac started to back off, but the snake struck at him from behind and he barely twitched out of the way. He pressed his back against the wall, wishing he could somehow pass through it.

A deep, echoing laugh filled the hallway. The snake hissed angrily in the direction of the sound, its head swaying back and forth, looking first at Zac, then down the hallway where the laughter continued. It bared its fangs at Zac once more, then receded into the statue's mouth.

The God-thing clenched its hands into fists as it was absorbed into the ceiling, where again it reached a benevolent finger toward the nascent Adam.

Footsteps echoed in the hall, and Zac turned to face their source. He heard laughter again as a figure emerged from the darkness.

"What do you want?" he croaked.

The laughter redoubled, and Zac saw the evil monk he had encountered at the temple, those same predatory eyes gleaming at him. Then the figure melted like candle wax, oozing and running, changing shape as Zac watched. An odor of mold and musk filled the air, and as the monk slowly re-formed himself into the Minotaur, the dizziness hit.

Too frightened even to be grateful, Zac reached out to

steady himself . . .

. . . and then he was lying in the grass, Cecile's tear-stained face hovering over him. Other faces hovered too, peering down at him. Someone was shouting to call an ambulance, and someone else was muttering, "Oh my God, oh my God."

Cecile hadn't said a word since they'd left the Gardens. She pulled the car into the parking lot now and stopped in front of Zac's apartment. "I don't see why you won't let me take you to the hospital," she said quietly, not looking at him.

Zac sagged back against the seat. "I can't explain it, Cecile. You're just going to have to believe me. I don't need a hospital. An asylum, maybe, but not a hospital."

"Zac, you were unconscious for five minutes! Something's wrong with you. What if you hadn't snapped out of it?"

"But I did! I always do!"

"Don't get angry with me! I'm trying to help you."

"I know, but . . . "

"But what?"

"But you can't help me with this."

"Then let me take you to someone who can! How about your brother? Maybe he can do something."

Zac shuddered at the very idea. He turned to look at her. "Cecile, George is the last person I would tell. Please don't get any funny thoughts about calling him behind my back or anything. He would do more harm than good."

"Zac—"

"Let me tell you about one of the times George 'helped' me. When I was in high school, this obnoxious bully, Pete, wanted me to steal a copy of an exam for him. I was a teacher's aide, so he knew I'd have access to her desk.

"Of course I refused, and of course he told me to meet him behind the gym after school. I guess teaching at a girls' school you don't get this sort of thing, but trust me, when you get called out, you have to go, or you'll be bully-bait the rest of your life.

"Well, word got around. Big Brother found out, and tried to convince me I shouldn't go. He was afraid I'd get in trouble. We don't do that in *our* family. But I was adamant: I'd rather have one drubbing and get it over with than have to look over my shoulder the rest of the school year.

"So George took matters into his own hands. He and some friends of his from the football team showed up behind the gym. George told Pete to lay off me, and Pete had to back down. Of course, I came home with bruises at least once a week for the rest of the year. See, George always thinks he knows what's best, but—"

"I'm not George," Cecile said. "I'm here for you. Why won't you talk to *me*? Please?"

Zac leaned his head against the headrest. She deserved the truth, but he knew what she'd think when she'd heard it. She'd be convinced she was dating a madman.

"Remember how you told me that nothing I could do or not do would make you love me any less?" Cecile asked. "What makes you think I feel any differently about you?"

She sounded so miserable. Zac could see in her face how much it hurt her to think that he didn't trust her.

"Cecile," he started, but could think of nothing to say.

Her voice turned icy. "Fine. If you won't go to the hospital, and you won't tell me what's wrong, you can just get out of the car."

The sudden anger in her voice was so startling that Zac could only stare at her. Her eyes told him this could be the last time he ever saw her. He put his elbows against the dashboard and lowered his face into his hands.

"I don't know . . . I can't begin . . . "

Cecile's anger melted and she put her hand on his back.

He didn't look up. He might manage to force the words out, but only an act of God could make him look at her as he told her. He swallowed hard and steeled himself for the effort.

"It started when I was in high school. I didn't have a lot of friends, and other kids made fun of me—or worse. Whenever things got particularly rough, I used to daydream about being the daring, outgoing type. I'd lie on my bed, close my eyes, and let my mind drift. I'd imagine adventures for myself, sort of like I saw in the movies, only with me as the hero.

"That was normal, I think, for a lonely kid. But then . . . things took a strange turn when I was a senior." He paused to gather his resolve. "I was reading *Hamlet* one afternoon after a really lousy day at school. I remember I had finally found the courage to ask this girl I liked to go to a movie with me, and she'd laughed at me. I don't think I've ever been so miserable in my life."

Until now, he thought.

"I couldn't concentrate on the play. I'd read a few lines, and then I'd think about what I would have done in Hamlet's place. Finally, I put the book down and closed my eyes, imagining what it would be like to be Hamlet. And as I was thinking about it, somehow it became more than a fantasy."

"What do you mean?" Cecile asked.

Zac licked his lips; his mouth had gone completely dry. "It's hard to explain. When you're fantasizing, it has a particular feel to it. You can lose yourself in the fantasy a bit, but you always know you're still sitting in your chair, still lying on your bed.

"This was different. I was *completely* unaware of my true surroundings. I was in Elsinore castle, and all I could see, hear, or feel was the castle. The people were real, real enough to reach out and touch. I overheard a couple of them talking about how Hamlet's father had been sighted, and then when they saw me they looked embarrassed and apologized, calling *me* Hamlet!

"I was terrified at first, but my fear faded quickly. I was in a place where exciting things were happening, and where I was at the center of it all. By the time I woke up—it turned out my mother was knocking on my door—I was so far from being afraid that I was disappointed to be yanked away.

"The next few days, nothing unusual happened. Nothing so unusual as finding myself suddenly in Denmark, anyway. But I did find myself longing to have that experience again, especially whenever I saw the girl who had laughed at me, or when some teacher would remind me how wonderful my brother had been when he went to my school. I wished I could return to Elsinore, where I was respected, and where I had control of my life and my destiny. I was convinced that in that fantasy, I had been in possession of my free will, that had I lived out the whole play, I would have been able to do things my way, not Hamlet's.

"So one day I sat down and tried to recreate the conditions that had sent me there the first time. I let my mind drift, thinking about the play but not concentrating, if you can understand that. And eventually it worked.

"I didn't stay long the second time; something pulled me out of it—the phone ringing, a dog barking, whatever—but when I woke up, I was ecstatic. I had willed myself to live a heroic fantasy so realistic it was indistinguishable from real life. There couldn't have been a better escape for a lonely, unhappy boy.

"As time went on, I found I could 'dream' myself into places other than Elsinore, exciting new worlds full of adventure. I've always thought of these dreams as 'Hamlet dreams,' though I haven't been back to Elsinore since."

Zac stopped and bit his tongue, trying to generate a little moisture. He didn't dare look to see how Cecile was taking this.

"For a while I thought the only happiness I would ever find was in the Other Place—that's what I call the place I go to when I dream. Then, I met you, Cecile. You made me happier than I'd ever been, and I stopped going to the Other Place so often. I still dreamed once in a while, when I'd had a particularly hard day, but it was a lot harder to get myself to drift, and the truth is, I didn't miss it.

"Then something changed. I found myself in the Other Place without even trying to go there. That was the other night, when you couldn't wake me up. It happened again last night, which is why I didn't go to work today. And it happened in the Gardens. I know it's the Other Place I'm going to—it all feels the same. But somehow, they're not dreams anymore; they're nightmares. And I don't come out of them so easily. I don't know what's happening or why. All I know is I'm scared."

He was finished.

Cecile said nothing; Zac hadn't thought she would.

"I'll go now," he said softly, hoping against hope that she would stop him. But her eyes glistened and stared straight ahead as he stepped out of her car.

3

Cecile woke with a start.

The nightmare again. It was coming more often lately.

She hadn't intended to sleep. She'd driven home from Zac's, closed herself in her room, and flopped onto her bed, overwhelmed. Was Zac sick? Insane? It was all too much for her.

Somehow she'd drifted off, and now it was almost bedtime—though she'd probably never get back to sleep. She sat up and took an aspirin.

A car door slammed in the parking lot. Cecile heard the footsteps on the stairs, heard the door of the apartment open, heard Panta's wild yips of pleasure.

Bess was home.

"Cecile?" Bess called from the living room, and Cecile sighed with frustration. Was there no way to find the solitude she desperately needed? The nightmares about Steve . . . Zac's revelation . . . Past and present merged to wring tears from her eyes, and she reached into her pocket for a tissue.

What she found instead was the yellow note from the bulletin board. *Cecile: I have not forgotten you.* And she remembered.

Her stomach lurched, and she dropped the note to the

floor. He had said that, when he was convicted. He had said he wouldn't forget her. Time had dulled her memory of the terror she had felt at that moment. But now she knew. It was Steve. It was Steve.

In a moment Bess was in the room and had her arms around Cecile, who was shivering uncontrollably.

"Cecile, honey, what's the matter? Talk to me." Bess held her, and for a moment Cecile could only cling, the pain of the day too much to bear. "Please Cecile, tell me what's wrong."

Unable to force words from her throat, Cecile picked up the note and thrust it into Bess's hands.

She read it and frowned. "I don't get it."

Cecile's voice came out a raspy whisper. "Somebody left that for me at school today. Steve. He said he wouldn't forget me."

Understanding dawned on Bess's face. "This is from him?"

Cecile nodded, fighting down another wave of hysteria.

"God. Did you see him?"

"No, but I told you. He said he wouldn't forget me."

"But that was what? Nine or ten years ago? Are you absolutely sure he wrote this?"

"It's him. I know it's him."

Bess took Cecile's hand and squeezed it. "You'd think if he were going to come looking for revenge he'd have done it when he got out of jail."

"My mom hired a private investigator to keep an eye on him right after he got out."

"And?"

"He moved somewhere. Texas, I think. That was the last we heard."

"Well, he's come an awful long way to leave you an anonymous note. There's no one else who might have left it?"

"I . . . I can't think of anyone."

"But it *could* be from someone else. And it *could* mean anything. Or nothing."

Cecile looked again at the note. Had the stress of this day colored her judgment? Why *would* Steve come after her after all this time?

The panic began to recede.

"Cecile, if you could see how pale your face is . . . "

"I don't need to see. I can feel it. Please, Bess. I need to be alone for a while."

"I suspect that's exactly what you *don't* need. Tell you what, let's call Zac and ask him to come over."

There was a sudden hollow feeling in the center of Cecile's chest, and her voice shook when she answered. "No. When I said I wanted to be alone, I really meant alone." Her words sounded flat and dull; Bess noticed, and nodded sagely.

"A fight? No wonder you're so upset. Well, you'll be happy to know I won't pry—but I do want to tell you about something that happened today. I promise, I'll tell you this little incident, then I'll go away." Bess flashed her most winning smile. It was almost enough to prompt Cecile to smile back. "I met this guy today."

Cecile groaned.

"Just hear me out," Bess laughed. "I'd never seen him before—he just moved into this complex a few days ago. And he asked about you, asked if you were my roommate. Cecile, he's one of the most gorgeous creatures I've ever seen!"

Cecile sat up and grasped Bess's hand. "My God, Bess! Was he tall? With light blonde hair?"

Bess frowned. "He was sort of tall, but his hair was so dark it was almost black. Why?"

"He could have dyed his hair," Cecile whispered.

"Oh. No, it wasn't Steve. He was much too young."

"Steve looks younger than he is. And there are plenty of

women who would think Steve is gorgeous."

"Cecile, it wasn't Steve! This guy couldn't be much older than you are. Unless your mom married a teenager, this is not the same guy!"

Cecile nodded. Steve *would* be about 40 now. "I'm being paranoid," she said. She took a deep breath and tried to let the tension flow out of her as she exhaled.

They sat together in silence a few moments. Then Bess patted Cecile's back and stood up. "Well, kiddo, I promised I'd leave you alone after I told you my news, so I'll make good on it. I'm sorry it scared you. I think you should forget everything else and enjoy having a secret admirer. And if you need to talk, you know where to find me."

Cecile managed a feeble smile, and Bess left, shutting the door after her and hesitating outside. Finally, Cecile heard the sound of receding footsteps. Only then did she lower her head into her hands.

Zac stood in the middle of a wobbly rope bridge suspended over an underground lake of blue water so clear he could see to the very bottom. He was inside an immense, desolate cave. Blue lights sparkled in the depths of the lake, and stalagmites reached up like great spears, waiting to impale anyone unlucky enough to fall into the water.

The bridge was about 150 feet long. It was anchored on the edge of the lake, and stretched across to a pitch-black opening in the cave wall. Something about the absolute black of that opening repulsed Zac, and he backed away. The bridge teetered as he did so, and he had to clutch at the rails to keep from falling off.

Holding on firmly, he made his way toward the shore of the lake, the bridge shimmying with every step. Why he wanted to reach that shore he didn't know, except that it would get him farther away from the menacing darkness at the other end of the bridge.

There was an unnerving, deathly silence to this place, and the shore of the lake was nearly devoid of light. Zac squinted into the darkness. Several tunnels led away from the lake, presumably into the depths of the cave, though one or more of those tunnels might also lead outside.

He shrugged and approached the leftmost tunnel, pausing to look in, hoping to see some sign of sunlight; but the tunnel curved sharply to the left only a few feet in. The only illumination came from two strings of dim blue lights that lined the walls of the tunnel.

As Zac set foot into the tunnel, the sound of a throat clearing startled him. He whipped around. Standing by the edge of the lake, leaning against the bridge, was Ariadne.

She wore the same cloak he remembered from the labyrinth, and also the same insulting smirk. Zac saw no way she could have sneaked up on him, unless she came from the darkness across the bridge or from the waters of the lake itself.

"So, you're just going to choose a tunnel at random and go waltzing in with no idea what may be waiting for you along the way?" she asked.

Zac scowled. "I don't see that I have an alternative."

"You rejected my help in Crete, and look how that turned out."

"I wasn't aware that you were offering any help."

Ariadne laughed. "No, I don't suppose you were."

"If you really want to help me," Zac said, "you can start by telling me what's happening to me. How am I coming here against my will? Are you bringing me here?"

"Hardly. I have neither the power nor the motive. But someone else has both. I suppose you have the right to know that you have an enemy here."

"An enemy? What do you mean? The Minotaur?"

"The Minotaur is a teddy bear," she laughed. "Your enemy is called Carcajou. He rules here. Our very own King Minos."

"So what have I done to him?"

Ariadne sat down on the edge of the bridge, dangling her toes in the water. "You didn't do anything, in particular. You entered his kingdom. Now he's aware of you and he doesn't want you to leave."

"Why not? What am I to him?"

Ariadne's face took on a strange expression, as if she'd just felt a sudden jolt of exultation and was trying to hide it. Her eyes glowed and she pressed her lips together to suppress a smile. "You are nothing to him. And everything. What matters is that to get out of here you must win your way out."

"Meaning what?"

"Do you need me to hand everything to you on a platter?" She kicked at the lake, sending a splash of ice cold water all the way to the center of Zac's chest.

"Hey!" he yelled in protest.

She looked up to meet his eyes, a sultry smile on her lips; then she stood, allowing her cloak to slide off her shoulders. She was naked underneath.

Zac caught his breath and quickly looked away. He heard Ariadne's laugh, then a splash as she dove into the lake. Almost against his will, he turned to watch her. Her fiery hair wrapped itself around her arms and chest and waist as she swam away from him toward the dark boundaries of his vision. Then she dove deep into the water, her long legs flashing into the air like a mermaid's tail. He watched as she swam the whole way back underwater.

Reaching the shore, she burst out of the water with a rush of bubbles and stood dripping before him, smoothing her hair back from her face. Zac couldn't keep from staring at her, at the tightness of her belly, the faint lines her ribs created through her skin, her full, round breasts.

Slowly, she moved in closer, running her tongue over the fullness of her lips. She stopped just short of him, close enough that he could feel the warmth of her breath on his throat, close enough that droplets of water streaming from her hair, over her shoulders, down her chest, dropped from her nipples and splashed on his feet.

"So," she murmured. "What do you want most? My help? Or something else?"

Zac trembled. Was she offering herself to him? Or just mocking him? She was so close. All he would have to do was twitch, and he would touch her, taste her lips, feel the perfection of her body. The temptation was so strong that he leaned toward her, ever so slightly.

Then he stopped himself with a jerk. He had told Cecile he would wait for her. Whether the Other Place was real or not was of no consequence. If he betrayed Cecile here, it was still a betrayal.

"You're the most beautiful woman I've ever seen," he whispered, "but you're not the one I want." He waited for her fury, for a slap across the face.

Ariadne's eyes turned hard and cold; then quickly the expression was gone, and she threw back her head and laughed. "Frankly," she said, "I doubt you'll get as good an offer anywhere else."

Somehow her words had no sting. He looked into her eyes, and wondered, would she have backed away if he had reached for her? Would he ever have managed to touch her? He doubted it. And if he had, he would have regretted it instantly.

He crossed his arms over his chest. "So," he said, "will you help me or not?"

"What would you do if I said 'not'?"

He shrugged. "Go down this tunnel, I suppose."

Ariadne rubbed her chin, as if deep in thought. "Well, then, I suppose I'll have to help you. None of these tunnels will lead you closer to Carcajou."

"Good!"

"You think so? You're enjoying your little journeys here so much that you wish them to continue, whenever he wishes to bring you here, whatever you happen to be doing and whoever you happen to be doing it with? If you want to be free of Carcajou, you must go to Carcajou. To get to him you must go the way he doesn't want you to go."

Zac's eyes strayed to the dark opening at the other end of the bridge.

Ariadne picked up her cloak from where it lay crumpled on the shore, and wrapped herself in it. "You can always tell the way he doesn't want you to go," she said. "It will be the way you least want to go. He is far from here, at the center of his labyrinth. You are at the very edge." She pointed at the darkness across the bridge. "That is the way to get deeper into the labyrinth, so he makes it dark, and bleak. Yet that is the way you must go."

"And if I go some other way?"

"You'll wander aimlessly, until Carcajou's will weakens and you awaken. It takes much of his strength to keep you here. But he regains his power quickly, and soon you'll be pulled in again, into another part of the labyrinth, still on its outer edges, still no closer to him, and you'll face this decision once more."

Zac shook his head. "And why is it that *you* want me to go deeper?"

"That's none of your concern."

"I want to know."

She paused, then said, "Not everyone calls me Ariadne. I have another name, one perhaps more appropriate." She looked at him expectantly.

"All right. What is this other name of yours?"

"Eris."

"Goddess of discord, if I'm not mistaken. So you're doing this for pure love of mischief?"

"What better reason?"

That she was lying, Zac had no doubt. The only question was where the lie began. Was she lying about Carcajou? About what would happen if he didn't go into that dark opening? About her own motives?

"You don't believe a word I've said, do you?" she asked. "Or at least you can't decide whether you believe it or not. All right. I have a bargain for you. Go into that tunnel you're so enamored of. Wander to your heart's content. Eventually, you'll awaken, and when you do, you'll discover an additional reason you might want to face Carcajou instead of indecisively twiddling your thumbs." There was a feral glee in her eyes now that sent a chill down his spine.

"What do you mean?"

"If I told you, you'd think I was lying. When you return, we'll talk again."

"Tell me what else you know!" he demanded, but Ariadne had already started across the bridge. It held steady beneath her feet, not swaying and rocking as it had for Zac. "Wait!" he shouted, but she only walked faster, and faded into the darkness at the other side.

Cecile watched Rose Stanhope carefully as the other girls filed one by one up to her desk and deposited their homework. Rose lagged at the back of the line, but didn't seem to be a part of it. She caught Cecile looking at her and smiled her most impudent smile. Then she tossed her head and made for the door. Cecile only briefly considered stopping her and demanding she turn in her homework. It would do no good, for Rose certainly hadn't done it, and Cecile wasn't up to a confrontation.

She gathered up the papers and stuffed them in her briefcase. How would she get herself to read them with all that was on her mind? Her teaching today had been dreadful—she had been distracted and absent-minded, her lectures rambling and uncertain.

She had slept badly last night. The lurking fear of Steve was part of it, but worse yet was the image of Zac's tortured face as he had gotten out of her car. He had trusted her with his deepest, darkest secret, and she had been too caught up in her own misery to reach out and help him. Zac had been so good to her, and this was how she repaid him.

Cecile's eyes started to burn. This was not the time or place for self-recrimination; she could wallow to her heart's content when she got home. Closing the classroom door behind her, she walked through the halls, praying she wouldn't run into Jerry, or Mrs. Stanhope, or Rose. She made it to her car unmolested, and as she drove through the gates of the school, she sighed heavily. The worst of the day was behind her.

She knew what she had to do. She couldn't leave Zac the way she had yesterday; she had to call him, to let him know that she was wrong and that she knew it. He loved her and he would forgive her.

He would have to see a doctor, of course. It was possible his symptoms were caused by something physical—maybe he had a brain tumor, or something. He was convinced he didn't need a doctor, though, and he could be so stubborn. Perhaps she could get him to talk to his brother. Keep it in the family.

Cecile sat in her car, outside her apartment, rehearsing in her mind the phone call she was determined to make. Then she hurried up the stairs and inside. She dropped her briefcase on the floor beside her bedroom door and sat down on the couch, ignoring Panta's demands of attention. At least Bess wasn't home. One less obstacle to face. Imagine what Bess would think of all that Zac had said yesterday!

She hesitated a moment as her hand reached out for the phone, then shook off her last doubts and dialed. The phone rang ten times before she gave up.

Biting her lip, she looked at her watch. Maybe Zac was at work. No, he wouldn't have gone to work today. He had been too distraught last night, and his job didn't mean that much to him. Had he gone out for groceries? Was he in the shower? Or was he lying unconscious on his floor, his mind captive to that strange fantasy world he had created for himself?

Wait an hour, she told herself. If you call him then and he doesn't answer, you'll go over in person and let yourself in.

She picked up her briefcase and settled herself on the sofa to grade the girls' homework. They were used to her diligence and she wouldn't let them down, even now. Other teachers might take days to return homework, but she would not. Panta whimpered softly at Cecile, then lost interest and trotted over to the door.

Just as Cecile pulled out the stack of papers, there was a knock on the door, and her heart fluttered. Maybe it was Zac! Maybe he was coming to her to try to make things right. She fairly leapt to her feet and hurried to look through the peephole, pushing the excited Panta aside. Her heart fell; it wasn't Zac, but a man she had never seen before.

She opened the door, leaving the chain on. Panta darted

toward the opening, but Cecile blocked his path with her foot. "Yes?" she asked. As she got a better look, she realized who this stranger had to be. He was tall and thin, with pitch-black hair slicked back into a short ponytail at the nape of his neck. Piercing dark eyes peered out of an angular face. The black t-shirt he wore was tight enough to show the ripple of muscles across his chest. He smiled at her, showing bright white teeth that were perfectly straight and even. He was—just as Bess had described him—one of the most gorgeous creatures she'd ever seen.

"Hello," he said. "I hope you don't think I'm being terribly pushy, but I moved here just a few days ago and I wanted to introduce myself."

Cecile blinked at him, at a loss for words. His dark blue eyes twinkled in amusement, but he seemed unperturbed by her silence, smiling his wolfish smile.

"I spoke to your roommate just the other day; Bess did at least mention me to you, I hope? I'm Carl." He stuck his hand under the chain and past the door.

Cecile dumbly shook his hand. It was cold and dry, with a firm, but not crushing, grip. Did she imagine it, or had he purposely caressed her palm at the end of that handshake? She swallowed hard, more unnerved by this self-possessed stranger than by anyone she had ever met.

Fighting to find something to say, Cecile noticed Bess's car pulling into the parking lot. Surely Bess would break this spell of awkwardness.

Carl followed the direction of Cecile's gaze and saw Bess getting out of the car. "Ah," he said, "your roommate arrives. Perhaps now you'll have to take the chain off your door."

Cecile blushed at the remark.

Making her way up the stairs toward the second-floor apartment, Bess said, "Well, I see you've deprived me of the pleasure of introducing you."

Carl laughed. "I told you I wasn't the world's most patient person."

"So you did," Bess replied. "Would you like to come in for a while?"

"That's the most welcome invitation I've had all day."

Irritated, Cecile closed the door, unhooked the chain, and scooped Panta up so he wouldn't slip out or get stepped on. With a sigh, she opened the door once more.

Carl stepped aside, politely allowing Bess to enter first, then made as if to follow her in. He stopped with one foot in the doorway and looked into Cecile's eyes. She found herself trapped by his gaze.

"I'm being terribly rude," he said. "Perhaps this is a bad time. I'll leave you in peace, if you prefer."

For a moment, Cecile couldn't answer. She did want to be alone with her thoughts, but she had a sense that something momentous was happening. "No, no," she heard herself saying, "please come in."

His eyes lingered on her a moment longer. Then he went inside, and she was able to look away. Her pulse raced in her throat and her hands were clammy. What was the matter with her? She could see that this was not Steve. Still, there was something about him . . .

Carl sat down on the middle seat of the sofa and Bess seated herself on the easy chair, leaving nowhere for Cecile to sit except right beside Carl on the couch. It had seemed like a casual action on his part, collapsing into the most convenient seat, but the grin he aimed at her showed that he knew exactly what he had done. And she had thought Jerry was pushy!

"Would you like something to drink?" she asked, refusing to let him win his little game. "I think we have some Coke in the fridge."

"Coke would be great," he replied.

Putting Panta down, she ducked into the kitchen, taking that opportunity to wipe her sweaty palms on her skirt. With Carl momentarily out of sight, it seemed easier to breathe, and her pulse calmed. She remembered feeling the same way when Jerry had begun to pursue her at school—what woman wouldn't enjoy, at least a little, the attention of a gorgeous guy? But Carl was far more arresting, more mysterious. Everything about him, from his slicked-back hair, to his sharp features, to his dark clothing, matched her ideal of beauty. She bit her lip as she poured the Coke. What could he possibly want with someone like her?

When Cecile returned to the living room, Carl had moved onto the lefthand seat of the couch. Panta was curled up on his lap, eyes closed in ecstasy as Carl scratched behind his ears. Even her dog was conspiring against her! Wordlessly, she handed Carl his drink, unnerved by the intensity with which he regarded her.

Bess aimed a self-satisfied smirk at Cecile, then stood and stretched, faking a yawn. "I've had a long day," she said. "I hope you'll forgive me, but I'm going to go to my room and nap for a little while."

"We'll forgive you if you'll promise to join us another time," Carl answered with a knowing grin.

Cecile gave Bess her most withering glare, but to no effect. "Come on, Panta," Bess beckoned. "Keep me company for a while." She reached out her hands, but Panta didn't open his eyes until Carl stopped scratching his ears and gave him a nudge. Resigned, the dog jumped down and allowed Bess to carry him away.

"Alone at last," Carl said when Bess was gone.

"What do you mean by that?"

"It's you I'd like to get to know better, not Bess."

"Remember you were worried about being pushy?"

Carl nodded.

"Well, you're being pushy."

He laughed. "Please forgive me. I'm afraid it's in my nature. Listen, if it makes you uncomfortable to be alone with a total stranger in your living room, we could go somewhere else. Maybe you'd like to get a cup of coffee? There's a lovely little coffee shop just two blocks from here, though I suppose you know that."

"I don't drink coffee," she lied.

"Tea, then. Come on, my treat." He sensed her hesitation as she struggled for some plausible, polite excuse. "Listen, I know I've made a mistake already by coming to your home. I should have waited for Bess to introduce us. Then I could have asked you out for coffee and you wouldn't be so nervous about it. But the coffee shop's a nice public place, and I promise we won't be gone long. What do you say?"

Cecile could see no polite way to get rid of him. "All right. But I'll hold you to that promise. I have a lot of homework to grade before tomorrow morning."

"Fair enough," he said, and smiled hugely at her. His eyes locked with hers once more. In his pupils, she could see her own image reflected back at her, and deep behind that, something else, something she couldn't name, something that made her go hot, then cold, in quick succession. Then he blinked, and it was gone.

Shaken, she followed him to the door.

4

A wisp of wind caressed Zac's cheek. The sensation startled him. A bird? He felt it again, like the touch of a soft hand, and he whirled around. No one was there. Nothing. He shrugged and stepped forward, following the dimly lit tunnel through its twists and turns.

Something (Someone?) yanked on his pants leg, then touched his shoulder. "Ariadne?" he called. He quickened his pace, though he could see only a few yards ahead. Again came the tugging on his pants, more insistent now, holding him back, grabbing, clinging, tearing at his clothes.

"Let go!" he shouted, kicking out with his free leg, flailing with his arms as if caught in a swarm of bees. His limbs met with nothing but air; yet he could not free himself.

His left arm was clutched, tightly. He batted at it wildly with his right hand, even as his legs were grasped, held, pulled, and still he could see nothing, could touch nothing. He was being dragged forward, by a dozen—hands?—each grip firm, unshakeable, as he struggled against the inexorable pressure.

Ahead, the tunnel came to a T. From the left side, Zac could see bright light—sunlight! He stopped resisting, conserved his strength. Then, just as he reached the T, with a deafening roar he bolted toward the light, tearing free, stumbling clumsily but quickly regaining his balance, continuing toward the light. It wasn't far. He could only hope his attackers would be unable to follow him outside the cave.

Something latched onto his leg. "No!" he shouted, struggling forward. He was almost there! Just a little farther! He would not be dragged back into the darkness!

The sunlight was blinding, but Zac's eyes adjusted quickly, and as he approached the end of the tunnel, he could see straight across to a soaring snow-crowned cliff, its top piercing the clouds. Between him and that cliff, there was no path, no ground, no bridge. Only a precipice that had no visible bottom. His heart froze at the thought that he had almost run out of the cave blindly.

Then, the tugging and pushing began again, not pulling Zac back toward the dark side of the T, but propelling him toward the precipice.

"No!" he shouted. "Ariadne! Help me!" But there was no answer, and though he struggled and flailed and dug in his heels, he was dragged closer and closer to the edge, until his toes hung over the ledge. Then, he was released.

Relief flooded him momentarily but as he tried to regain his balance, windmilling his arms wildly, he felt his weight slowly tipping forward. His feet lost contact with the ledge, and with a dizzying lurch, he fell.

Cecile squirmed under Carl's scrutiny. His eyes bored into her, intense and demanding. She tried to think of things to say, anything to break the silence, the tension. Carl himself seemed completely at ease, not disconcerted in the least by the dearth of conversation.

"Are you enjoying your tea?" he asked suddenly.

"It's very good," she answered, though she had barely

noticed the flavor.

"How about the company?" He grinned at her and leaned slightly forward.

Cecile sighed and put her cup down. It was time she asserted just a little control over the situation. "Carl, what do you want from me? I mean, we just met."

He laughed. "Ever hear of love at first sight?"

She snorted.

"You don't believe in it, I guess," he said. "Well, maybe I don't either. But I feel something between us, a kind of chemistry. I felt it the first time I saw you. If you don't feel it yet, that's fine. I'm just asking you to give me a chance."

"Carl, I already have a boyfriend." She thought of what Zac was going through and felt a rush of guilt.

"Lucky guy!" Carl flashed her a rueful smile. "All right. I can take a hint. But we can still be friends, can't we?"

Cecile hesitated.

"At least friendly neighbors?" he pressed.

"That sounds fair enough," she said. She wondered just how "friendly" Carl intended to be.

He reached his hand over the table. "Friendly neighbors, then," he said. "Let's shake on it."

She took his hand, and a jolt of electricity passed through his palm into hers. Every nerve in her body came alive and tingled. She sat transfixed by his gaze as slowly he raised her hand. The warm, damp touch of his lips to her knuckles almost stopped her heart. Then he let go, and she was free to move again. Quickly, she pulled her hand away and, under the table where he couldn't see, rubbed the spot he had kissed against her skirt.

"We can be 'friendly neighbors,'" he said, "but that doesn't mean I have to give up *all* hope. If things don't work out with your boyfriend . . . "

"I need to go home now," she said, barely managing a whisper.

Zac opened his eyes. Frantically he reached out and grabbed the arms of his favorite chair, convinced he was still falling, his head spinning from vertigo. He held on tightly a few tense moments, then let out his breath and released his grip.

Groaning, his neck cramped and stiff, he sat up and saw his coffee cup shattered on the floor, splatters of coffee spotting the dingy carpet. The coffee had dried, and sunlight was streaming through the window; he had been out a long time.

Afraid, but needing to know, he looked at his watch. Only five o'clock! Then he realized it was too bright to be five in the morning. He had been in the Other Place more than twelve hours! And if Ariadne was right, if this Carcajou person (if indeed he was a person) had the power to pull Zac into the Other Place at will, it might not be long before he passed out again.

One thing was certain: he couldn't face this alone. And if the only way he could win back Cecile's confidence was to see a doctor, he would just have to see a doctor. He might well find himself on Thorazine, but anything would be better than this.

First, though, he had to talk to Cecile. He picked up the phone and dialed. After two rings, Bess answered.

"May I speak to Cecile, please?" Zac asked, hearing how thin his voice sounded in his ears.

"Zac?"

"Yes."

"Cecile's not here. Can I take a message for her?"

"Listen, I know she's upset with me right now, but I really need to talk to her. Please tell her I need her help."

"I'm sorry, Zac, she's really not here. I'm not trying to put you off. I do know something happened between you two, but she hasn't told me what it was, and she certainly hasn't said anything about not wanting to talk to you. I promise."

"Do you know when she'll be back?"

"No, I couldn't say. She's gone out with a new neighbor of ours, Carl. They'll probably be back soon, but you never know."

Zac said nothing. Was Bess was making this up? She had made no secret of her personal opinion of Zac. Maybe she was inventing a mystery man to make Zac jealous, to drive a wedge between him and Cecile.

Then again, maybe Cecile was out with another man.

"Zac? You there?"

He cleared his throat. "Yes. Just ask her to call me when she comes in. Tell her it's very important."

He hung up the phone and bowed his head in despair. What if Cecile didn't call back? Who could he turn to? Was she already giving up on him?

Though he felt completely disinclined to eat, Zac's stomach was rumbling angrily, and there was no guarantee he wouldn't black out for another fourteen hours any second now. He opened the refrigerator . . .

. . . and found himself standing in a large, cluttered room with a high ceiling. "God, no!" he said. "Not already!" It hadn't been ten minutes.

Before him, carved of something grainy and white, was a huge head, wearing a winged helmet. He reached out and touched it. Styrofoam. The floor was dusted with white flakes that looked like a cross between snow and sawdust. He picked up a handful. It was Styrofoam also, and it clung to his skin and clothing.

All around him were stage settings, with gigantic statues

and mannequins, and to his left he saw several glass display cases holding life-sized figures. Curious, he stepped toward a display case in which stood a lifelike mannequin dressed as a geisha. She held an ornamental fan modestly over the lower portion of her face, though the twinkle in her eyes suggested she was smiling. Zac bent to read the plaque at the mannequin's feet. It was in Spanish, but he gathered that this costume had been used in a production of Puccini's "Madame Butterfly." The intricate embroidery on the mannequin's kimono suggested that this was a wealthy theater, to say the least.

Zac glanced upward once more as he was about to step toward the next display case, and stopped dead in his tracks. The mannequin was now holding her fan at chest-height. A cold tickle danced up his spine.

As he watched the geisha, Zac eye caught a glimmer of movement nearby. He started and glanced in that direction. In the next display case stood a statue of a knight in plate-mail armor. When Zac had first come in, the knight had been leaning on his sword, hadn't he? Yet now he held it raised.

Slowly, Zac backed away from the display cases, and bumped against a "stone" pillar that reached almost to the ceiling. It toppled to the floor. More Styrofoam.

There were several doors leading out of the room, each with a red "Salida" sign over it. Directly in front of one of those doors was another Styrofoam carving, this one of a three-headed dog. It was painted solid black—except for the eyes. All six eyes glowed red. Like the eyes on the painting of God that had threatened Zac.

Did he imagine it, or did one of the heads move ever so slightly? Just looking at that dog left him feeling queasy.

"I suppose you can guess which way Carcajou does not want you to go."

Zac swung around, and Ariadne stepped out from behind a half-painted oak tree. "I wish you'd stop sneaking up on me," Zac said, but he supposed she enjoyed startling him, seeing him jump.

"Did you have a nice trip home?" she asked, her voice honey-sweet.

He ignored her question. "You said that the next time I came here you would give me some reason why I would prefer to go in deeper."

"My, how you hang on my every word. Indeed I did. Did you get a chance to visit with your girlfriend while you were home?"

Zac blinked. How did she know so much about his real life? "Why do you want to know?"

She shrugged. "I have answers for you. But to get those answers, you must give me some yourself. Now, did you visit Cecile?" She put extra emphasis on that last word.

Zac resisted the urge to question her. "No," he said.

"And why not? Isn't she the very center of your universe? Isn't she the first one you want to see and talk to when you wake up?"

His fingers curled into fists at the mockery in her voice. "I tried to call her, but . . . " The words died in his throat as he realized what he was about to say.

Ariadne laughed, her eyes glittering with malice. "But she wasn't there. She was out, with another man. Who do you suppose that was, Hamlet?"

The blood drained from Zac's face as the implication of her words hit him. His heart clenched like a fist and for a moment it was all he could do to will himself to breathe.

"What's wrong, Hamlet? You don't like the idea of Carcajou fucking your girlfriend?" She seemed to relish her sudden vulgarity. "Well, it's going to happen, eventually. He's very . . . persuasive. And the longer you continue your Hamlet impersonation, sitting around with your thumb up your ass, the more time he has to work on her."

Zac was shaking. Could Cecile really be out with this enemy of his? Was Carcajou trying to seduce her? The whole idea was ridiculous! Carcajou was a figment of his imagination, certainly no danger to Cecile.

"I don't believe you," he said, trying more to convince himself than Ariadne.

"You mean you don't want to believe me. But if you believe that Carcajou can pull you here, as you must, then is it so hard to imagine that he can pass into your world?"

Zac took a deep breath. If this was true, if Carcajou was indeed trying to seduce Cecile, still it was impossible to believe he would succeed. Whatever his seductive power, Carcajou would never break down the walls that Cecile had built around herself.

"You're trying to convince yourself that you have plenty of time, that Cecile will resist all temptation just to wait for you. Go ahead and enjoy that illusion. But let me ask you something: do you love her?"

Zac could barely find his voice. "That's none of your business."

"Answer me anyway."

"Yes," he whispered, "I love her."

"And do you want me?"

"No!" he answered, far too quickly and too loudly.

Ariadne chuckled. "Liar. Of course you want me. I saw the evidence, so to speak, in the Labyrinth of Crete. It's not something you can hide when you're naked, I'm afraid. How long do you think you could resist me?"

"As long as I needed to."

"You're living in a fantasy world, dear. Even if you *are* as stout-hearted as you imagine, do you think Cecile is as strong? She will find Carcajou at least as seductive as you find me. With you popping in and out of her life at his will, how long do you think she'll last? And how do you suppose you'll feel when that which you most want has been given to someone else?"

"It's not 'that which I most want!'"

"Hmpf! So you say. But trust me on this: she doesn't stand a chance against him."

"You're wrong. You don't know her. She's very strong."

Ariadne shook her head, and her face took on a sympathetic expression as she reached out and put a hand on his shoulder. "Carcajou could find the weakness in anyone," she said gently. "That's what he's good at. No one is invulnerable. Not even I." For the first time, Zac saw something human in her eyes, something that looked like a deep, aching hurt.

"You asked me why I was helping you," she continued, "and I said it was out of mischief. That isn't exactly true." Her voice softened and her eyes glittered with a hint of repressed tears. "I have other motives—and no intention of sharing them with you. Suffice it to say that Carcajou is more dangerous than you can possibly know, and if you truly love Cecile, you won't leave her to fight him alone."

"If he's so strong and so dangerous, what can I possibly do to fight him even if I do reach the center of his labyrinth?"

Ariadne shook her head. "That part is your battle, not mine. If you can make it there, you may find the will to defeat him. It will be a struggle just to reach him. I told you, you are on the very outskirts of the labyrinth. He is a prism that rests in the center. He casts many reflections throughout the outer rings, and they will try to stop you at each step. You've met some of them already."

"The Minotaur?"

She nodded.

"And the monk?"

"They will get stronger as you advance. I do not tell you you will defeat Carcajou, but the longer you take, the longer Cecile remains in his clutches. And the less chance you have of escaping this place."

Suddenly, Zac felt dizzy. Ariadne reached out a hand to steady him.

"Fight it!" she said. "You've wasted too much time already. His strength builds every moment you're not progressing. You must start your journey."

Zac tried to shake her hand off, but she held firm. "I've got to warn Cecile." He tried to give in to the dizziness, to return to the real world, but a sudden, stinging slap from Ariadne dragged him back.

"Warn her of what?" she asked. "That a character from your fantasies has come to life and is dating her? There's nothing you could tell her that she would believe and fear."

Zac reached up and touched the cheek she had slapped. It burned terribly.

"I'm sorry," she whispered, shaking her head. "I shouldn't have done that. Please believe me. You *must* stay." She looked desperate beyond all explanation, and Zac wondered what it was that Carcajou had done to this self-assured, proud woman to make her want his defeat this badly, to make her beg for help from the likes of Zac. He no longer doubted her sincerity; for whatever reason, she wanted Carcajou to lose.

Feigning a confidence he did not feel, Zac stepped toward the Styrofoam Cerberus that guarded the exit.

Ariadne smiled. "Hamlet takes action at last."

They walked in silence. Carl was too close to Cecile: she could feel the heat of his body, smell the cinnamon coffee on his breath. As they reached the base of the stairs leading up to her apartment, she stopped with her foot on the first step. If she let him walk her to the door, he would somehow talk his way inside. She couldn't face that; it was time to make her stand.

"Thank you for the tea," she said. "I'd better get inside and get to work, or I'll be up all night." Her voice came out embarrassingly husky.

Carl leaned forward until his body was almost touching hers. Surprised, she looked up to meet his eyes. His lips were slightly parted, and he didn't smile. She could just make out the tip of his tongue as it moved between his teeth. He bent his head toward her, leaning in, nose inches from hers, as her heart raced. Her breathing came in short little gasps and she couldn't will herself to back away.

"Until the next time," he whispered.

She nodded, unable to speak, then turned and started up the stairs.

A sliver of moon emerged from the cloud cover. Cecile paused on the landing to collect her thoughts, then stepped inside the apartment and closed the door and rested her back against it, shutting her eyes tight. When she opened them, Bess was standing in front of her.

"Is something the matter?" Bess asked.

Cecile bit down on her anger, to keep her voice civil. "Bess, don't you *ever* do that to me again."

"Do what?" Bess asked with exaggerated innocence.

"You know perfectly well."

"I guess it wasn't such a hot first date, huh?"

"It wasn't any kind of a date! In case you've forgotten, I *have* a boyfriend."

"Zac! He just called."

"What? When?"

"Just before you came in. He wants you to call back—says it's real important."

"Thank God he's all right!"

Cecile started toward her room, but Bess called to her. "Cecile?"

"Yes?"

"I'm sorry if I'm being a pain. You know I'm just trying to help."

"I know," Cecile answered as she closed her bedroom door. She picked up the phone and dialed Zac's number. He'd told Bess it was important. Maybe he had decided to see a doctor after all.

She let the phone ring ten times before she hung up. Where was he now? Something had to be wrong, and Cecile knew what it was. She rushed through the living room, ignoring Bess, and out the front door.

Bess ran out behind her. "Cecile, what's the matter?"

"I can't talk now!" she shouted. She got into her car, slamming the door behind her.

Restraining herself from driving as fast as her car could go, Cecile took deep breaths to restore some semblance of calm. She would do Zac no good if she got stopped for speeding on the way over. Not that she could do much good anyway. Her efforts to rouse him in the Gardens had been fruitless. He had come out of it, but not because of anything she had done.

"Calm down, Cecile," she said aloud. "He could be perfectly fine. Maybe he was in the bathroom." She tried to take comfort in the thought, but to no avail.

Zac's car was in the parking lot. She pulled up beside it. Fumbling to find her key to his apartment, she hurried to the door. She didn't bother knocking, just unlocked the door and burst into the room.

Zac lay face down on the kitchen floor, the refrigerator door hanging open as cold air flooded the room. Cecile knelt beside him, crying. She turned him onto his back. A bruise was forming on his brow; otherwise he appeared simply to be sleeping, as he had in the Gardens. She could see his eyes moving behind his closed lids. She shook him hard. "Wake up, Zac," she sobbed. "I'm here. And I'm so sorry. Please wake up."

Hands shaking, she grabbed the kitchen phone and dialed 911 and summoned an ambulance. Then she noticed Zac's address book by the phone. She flipped though the book until her eyes lit on one name: George. She hadn't met Zac's brother, but she knew he was a psychiatrist. Maybe he could help. She dialed his number, praying he would be home.

A child's voice answered the phone. "May I speak to George Martins?" Cecile asked, her voice quaking.

"Daddy!" the child yelled, not bothering to cover the receiver.

"Katie, don't shout," a man's voice boomed from nearby. "Hello?" he said on the phone, much more softly.

"Hello," she said, fighting to keep her voice under control. "My name is Cecile Graham. I'm Zac's girlfriend."

"What's wrong?" he asked, alarmed.

"I don't know," she said. She started to cry. "He's out cold and I can't get him to wake up. I've called an ambulance."

"I'll meet you at the hospital!" he said brusquely, then hung up without another word.

Cecile sat down beside Zac and took his hand in hers as the wail of the siren grew louder.

Zac eyed the Styrofoam Cerberus suspiciously.

"What are you waiting for?" Ariadne asked. "I thought you'd made your decision."

He tuned her out. For now, nothing mattered but Cerberus and the door he guarded. Had the head closest to the door been baring so many teeth all along? He was sure he would have noticed those gleaming white canines; they didn't have the grainy look of the unpainted Styrofoam. Come to think of it, Cerberus seemed to be covered with fur, not with paint, and his hackles were slowly bristling, even as Zac watched. Aware of Ariadne lurking behind him, waiting to mock him should he falter, he moved a little closer. A low growl emanated from the nearest head and the other two heads slowly swivelled to face Zac, hate-filled eyes menacing him. A rivulet of sweat trickled down the small of his back.

"He can't actually hurt you, you know," Ariadne said from close behind. Zac kept his eyes fixed on the three-headed dog. "In this ring of the labyrinth, nothing can hurt you. When you go deeper, that will not be the case. Enjoy your safety while you have it."

"Do you want me to go on or don't you?" he snapped. He took a deep breath and continued toward the door. The creature's growl grew louder, all three heads now joining in, ears flattened, fangs bared. It crouched low as if ready to spring.

Zac was close enough now that he could have reached out to touch Cerberus had he wished. Still, though the guardian dog snarled and growled, it made no move to attack. Zac groped for the door knob and started to turn it as the dog stepped toward him, barking. Shoving the door open, Zac lunged through and kicked the door shut. He heard the thump of Cerberus's body against it.

He turned. He was standing in a dim alleyway, lit by a single, flickering street lamp. Rows of trash cans lined the alley, filling the air with the sour smell of rot. Puddles stagnated in the gutters. No light shone from any of the surrounding buildings, and those windows that were not boarded up were broken and grimed with dust and cobwebs. Zac thought he glimpsed a pair of eyes observing him through one of those broken windows, but when he blinked and looked more closely, the eyes were gone.

"Ariadne?" he called, his words sounding tinny in the empty alleyway. No answer, but he heard what sounded like a snicker, quickly suppressed. Behind him a trash can fell over with a crash, and Zac's heart leapt to his throat as he spun around.

Amid the scattered trash that had spewed from the fallen can sat a large rhesus monkey, rummaging through the trash, examining each piece in turn before throwing it over its shoulder. The monkey looked up from its work and met Zac's puzzled gaze. Then its lips split into something very like a human grin, and it laughed, an insane human laughter that continued to gush forth, echoing in Zac's ears, even as he backed slowly away.

The alleyway opened onto what looked like a major street. A median, covered with dandelions, which had matured beyond the flowering stage into white puff-balls, divided the four-lane street. These dandelions weren't just unruly weeds: they had been planted in orderly rows.

Directly across the street yawned the mouth of a parking deck, even more dimly lit than the alley had been. A single yellow bulb illuminated the first floor of the deck, and Zac could see no light whatsoever on the upper floors. A hollow feeling of dread settled in the pit of his stomach. That was the way Carcajou didn't want him to go, the way to the next level of the labyrinth.

From a nearby street came the sudden roar of engines, lots of them, getting closer.

Zac ducked back into the alleyway—the monkey seemed to have wandered off—and pressed himself against the wall in a pool of shadow, as fifteen or twenty motorcycles roared to a stop in front of the parking deck. The bikers looked like any "typical" biker gang, except that they were all dressed exactly alike: black, steel-tipped boots, dark blue jeans, black, studded leather jackets. Each had his hair pulled back into a ponytail. The bikers dismounted, forming a circle.

One man, larger and stronger-looking than the rest, strode into the center of the circle. He was wearing a spiky crown that might once have been a hubcap. He nodded briefly, and on that signal another man, his hands cuffed behind his back, was thrust into the center of the circle. The force of the shove sent him to his knees. Smiling grimly, the biker-king motioned to one of his minions. "Uncuff him," he said.

"Let me go!" the captive shouted from his knees, his voice sounding frightened rather than defiant. With the handcuffs off, he tried to rise.

The biker-king punched the captive in the stomach, and the man bent over double, then collapsed. One of the others dragged him to a street lamp, and his hands were cuffed once more behind him, around the lamppost. The bikers laughed as the captive struggled to his feet, then sank to his knees, sobbing.

"Larry, Larry," the biker-king said, "Is this display really necessary? Have a little self-respect."

"Please," Larry cried, "there's still time to find a proxy."

The biker-king looked at an imaginary watch. "No, I'm afraid not. Your time is up."

"I'm so sorry your proxy escaped!" one of the other bikers said, utterly insincere.

"You let him go, you bastard!" Larry screamed, struggling against the cuffs that now drew blood from his wrists. "Next time, it'll be you!"

"Not me: I'm not stupid enough to let someone else guard

my proxy."

A gust of wind swept through the dandelions in the median, creating a swirling mist of tiny white seeds. Then, a long, high-pitched wail sounded from the depths of the parking deck. The hair on the back of Zac's neck prickled at the sound. The bikers as one stopped laughing and turned their heads toward the deck. The wail sounded again, joined by other voices. Hurriedly, the gang remounted their bikes, Larry pleading with them to free him. They ignored him and rode off. Every instinct in his body told Zac that he too should flee, but the alley was a dead end, and he dared not enter the street.

For a moment after the roar of engines had faded, there was utter silence, as Larry stared horror-stricken into the deck. Then the chorus of wails swelled once more. Huddling deeper into the shadows, Zac watched several ghostly figures emerge from the depths of the parking deck.

There were ten or twelve of them: emaciated, white-skinned, white-haired wraiths, with burning eyes set deep in hollow-cheeked faces, keening as they approached. Gossamer white rags partially clothed their frail bodies. When their eyes fixed on Larry, the mournful wails became cries of exultation.

The wraiths circled the captive biker. Blood flowed in earnest from his wrists as he tried desperately to free himself. He kicked savagely at the wraith nearest him, but his kick barely knocked it back and seemed to hurt it not at all.

One wraith knelt behind Larry, seizing his elbows to keep him still. Its long black tongue snaked out of its mouth and lapped at the blood on his wrists. The others were upon Larry now, touching him everywhere, black tongues flickering. One put its mouth to his, in a mockery of a kiss. One used first its claw-like nails, then its teeth to tear away the fly of his jeans.

For a moment, Larry seemed dazed, submitting to the licks and caresses with no struggle. Then the wraith behind him drew back its lips, revealing long white teeth that looked like they belonged in the mouth of a large dog. It sank its teeth deep into Larry's wrist, and he screamed in pain and terror. The other wraiths began to wail again, as one by one they, too, bared their teeth and sank them into his flesh.

Zac covered his mouth with his hand and closed his eyes. His knees buckled, and he dropped to the ground and wrapped his arms around his head to block out the hideous noises, knowing he should be running headlong from the horror before him.

The screaming soon stopped, though the cries of the wraiths grew louder and more exultant. Other sounds were even harder to bear: crunching and tearing noises that wormed their way into Zac's head. Eventually, these sounds, too, ended, and the wailing of the wraiths began to fade.

Shivering uncontrollably, Zac opened his eyes. The last of the wraiths were receding from view, drifting into the darkness of the parking deck, their ecstatic cries dissolving into the air.

Zac's stomach heaved as he looked at the lamppost. There was nothing left but the handcuffs.

"So how do you like this level of the labyrinth so far?" Ariadne's voice purred from behind him.

The horror of what he had witnessed was so intense that Zac didn't even start at the sound of her voice. His mouth was so dry he couldn't speak.

"You're looking a little green, Hamlet dear. I hope you don't think you've seen the worst the labyrinth has to offer."

She drifted past him, out to the median where the wraiths had had their grisly feast, and picked one of the dandelions, carrying it back to where Zac stood, still motionless and speechless, as if he had been turned to stone.

"They can rend flesh from bones as easily as this," she said, blowing a flutter of seeds into his face. "And to have any chance of winning your freedom and saving your lady love, you must go in there." She turned toward the parking deck.

"No," Zac whispered. The paralysis finally released his limbs and he ran, away from Ariadne, away from the wraiths, away from Carcajou, and away, a part of him knew, from his only hope.

5

The back of the hard plastic chair bit into Cecile's shoulder blades as she leaned her head against the wall and closed her eyes. The drone of the waiting room filled her ears: the echoing of the intercom; the worried whispers of friends and relatives; the squeak of the nurses' rubber soles on the tile floor. She even thought she could hear George's voice booming out from somewhere.

George had taken charge the moment he had arrived, declaring himself Zac's next of kin and effectively knocking Cecile out of the loop. Not that she minded much. The barrage of doctors' questions that had assailed her when she had arrived with Zac had been more than she could bear. Trying to explain what had been happening lately, what Zac had told her about his episodes, had strained her almost to the breaking point.

Then George had arrived, and suddenly everything was out of her hands. The only attention he had granted her thus far was to recriminate her bitterly for telling the doctors about Zac's fantasy life.

"Now they'll declare him a mental case," he had fumed. "They'll run a few tests—some X-rays and blood work, maybe even a CAT scan—but in the end, they'll call it a psychiatric problem, and they won't have to deal with it anymore."

"Well—" Cecile had started, but George had dismissed her with a wave.

She didn't regret telling the truth. Maybe the evidence of Zac's fantasy life would give the doctors what they needed to cure him.

The sound of approaching footsteps prompted her to open her eyes. George stood before her, looking less self-assured than he had when he had first blustered in. She sat up straight as he took the seat next to her.

"They have no idea what's wrong with him," George said, shaking his head. "To all appearances, he's asleep. His EEG is consistent with a person in REM sleep. His blood work is normal. His X-rays are normal. The CAT scan didn't show anything. But they can't get him to wake up. They've got a neurologist in there now, but he's already convinced that it must be something psychological. I wish you . . . Never mind, it doesn't matter. They'd be calling in a psychiatrist by now anyway. At least I convinced them to look for a physical cause first."

Cecile resisted an intense urge to retort. The doctors had seemed to her quite willing to look for a physical cause, even after what she had told them. They had of course asked her about his psychiatric history, and whether he had a drug or alcohol problem that she knew of, but she had sensed no condescension in their manner.

She took a calming breath before allowing herself to speak: "What happens next?"

"The Neurology department pokes around at him for a couple of days; and then they send him off to Psychiatry. Then . . . well, I'll worry about that later."

"Do *you* think it's a psychiatric problem?"

George sighed. "I don't know. The fact is, Zac and I have

never been close. I see him, what, maybe once or twice a year, and when I do see him, we usually fight. I know nothing about what's going on in his life or in his head. He's always seemed a little strange, but it never occurred to me that there might be something *wrong* with him."

Cecile bristled at his tone. "He's not here because of a character flaw."

"I didn't mean that. It's just . . . How long have you known my brother?"

"About six months."

"I've known him since he was born. And he's been 'different' all that time. He used to get picked on a lot because of it. He probably doesn't even remember that I used to stick up for him, often to my own detriment."

"So what are you trying to say?"

"I'm saying that I'll stick up for him even now. I've never been able to understand him, nor him me, but he's still my brother."

"Have you called your parents?"

"No. They'd only worry. I'll call them when I know more about his condition."

"Surely they would want to know!"

George shook his head. "There's nothing they can do for him, and it's not like he's all alone. I'll make sure the doctors take good care of him."

"And where does that leave me?" Cecile asked.

"Forgive me for saying it, but I don't know. Zac's never said a thing about you to anyone in the family, as far as I know. And to tell you the truth, I'm not sure how much of this is really any of your business."

"Any of my business!" Cecile sprang to her feet, so stung she wanted to slap him in the face. "I've watched this happen to him. I've been there when he suddenly stopped living in the same reality that I do. He told me his deepest, darkest secret, and I threw it back in his face! That's the last time I saw him conscious. I would kill myself if he never woke up and that was the last memory he had of me. How dare you say it's not my business! I love him!"

George's mouth hung slightly open. He looked for all the world like his loveable pet bunny had just bitten him. Cecile herself was startled by the ferocity of her retort. She, who took every insult meekly, then cried about it when she was alone, had actually shouted at George!

George rose to his feet. At six foot two, he towered over her. "I'm sorry," he said, much to her amazement. "You're right, of course. What happens to Zac is certainly your business, and I should be thanking you for calling me as soon as you did. I've just never been able to see straight where my brother is concerned. I shouldn't have taken my frustrations out on you."

"I'm sorry too. It's not like me to lose my temper. It's been a long and terrible day."

"Why don't you go on home. There's nothing more either of us can do here. If you give me your phone number, I'll call you the moment I have any news." He handed her a pen and one of his business cards, and she scrawled her phone number. Then he took the card from her and strode out of the waiting room without another word.

Despite George's assurances, Cecile had remained in the waiting room two more hours. Now it was nearing midnight as she parked in front of her building. The light was on in her apartment; Bess had waited up, not surprising considering how abruptly Cecile had run out. Bess was undoubtedly worried about her, but how could Cecile explain Zac's condition yet again, and to the person least likely to be sympathetic?

A Corvette pulled into the neighboring parking space just as Cecile opened her car door. She got out and locked the door, and by the time she had turned around, Carl was standing at her side.

"Well," he purred, "fancy meeting you here. Do you live around here?"

Cecile managed a smile as weak as the joke. "I—"

"Getting in awfully late, aren't we?" He glanced pointedly at his watch. "Must have had a hot date."

"Not exactly," she said, glancing longingly at the stairs. Carl was blocking her way, leaning against his car and stretching his long legs all the way over to hers.

"What a pity. Both of us coming in at midnight, and neither one having had a hot date. Who would believe it, eh?"

"Listen, Carl. I'm tired, and—"

"Nothing a good cup of coffee won't cure. Oh, I forgot. You don't drink coffee. Well, tea has much the same effect. May I offer you a cup? My apartment's just over there." He pointed with his chin.

"Thank you, but—"

"I insist. Come on." He stood up straight and offered her his elbow, smiling crookedly.

She eyed him suspiciously. He was a lot bigger than she was, and he looked very strong. What if his "charm" turned to something else when he was refused? She had no illusion that she could fight him off. But then, all she had to do was scream. Bess was still awake up there.

She took a step toward the stairs, and Carl blocked her way, trying to make it look accidental. "Now, you're not going to turn me down, are you?" he asked.

"I'm sorry, Carl. I—"

"Perhaps you'd like something a bit stiffer than tea," he suggested. "You look a little pale and stressed out. How about a brandy?"

"I don't drink," Cecile said as the edges of panic beset her. Carl was not going to let her go by.

"You don't drink coffee, you don't drink brandy, you barely touch tea. What *do* you do?"

"Let me go," she whispered.

"I'm hardly forcing you to stay," he told her. But he was. His eyes held her motionless. "If you really want to go, just walk on by. I'm just trying to offer a more appealing option."

"Cecile?"

Cecile looked up. Bess had come out and was standing on the landing. Bess would rescue her.

"I've been so worried about you!" Bess said. "What happened? Where have you been?"

Cecile glanced at Carl. He had moved aside enough to let her by and he was staring up at Bess. His face was overtly expressionless, but there was something about the glint in his eyes that sent a chill through Cecile.

His attention snapped back to Cecile as she slipped by him. "Well, then, goodnight," he whispered.

Cecile nodded briefly without looking at him and practically raced for the stairs. She stepped through the doorway and into the apartment, making a beeline for the couch and allowing Bess to lock up behind her.

"Maybe you're right about that guy," Bess said as she fastened the chain. "There's something creepy about him. I saw from the window the way he had you cornered there."

"Thanks for coming out, Bess. I don't know what would have happened if you hadn't."

Bess sighed deeply and sat beside Cecile on the couch, tucking her feet up under herself. "This is all my fault," she said. "I shouldn't have pushed him on you. Somehow, when I met him, he just seemed charming and gorgeous."

"What will I do if he doesn't leave me alone?"

"Just tell him you're not interested, in no uncertain terms. Some men need the big stick method to get the hint."

"You're right. I need a little more backbone. It's just . . . there's something about him that . . . makes it so hard."

Bess frowned. "All right. Never mind about him right now. Tell me what's going on."

Knowing she didn't own a stick big enough to make Bess take no for an answer, Cecile settled in to give a carefully edited account of the night's events.

How long he'd been wandering, Zac didn't know, but it was full night once more. He had experienced several fleeting hints of dizziness, and had seized on them, trying—in vain—to shift back to the real world. Now he hunkered down in the shadowy area between two stoops to rest his feet and legs.

Besides the bikers, the only people he had seen had been moving so furtively that he might almost have thought them to be ghosts. He could only assume they were trying to avoid the attention of the bikers, and, wishing ardently to do the same, he had kept low and hidden.

His attempts to find food and water had been wasted, and he would soon be dehydrated. Even now, his stomach rumbled angrily as he closed his eyes and leaned his head against the wall behind him. He would rest just a few minutes . . .

The roar of motorcycle engines jolted him awake. He glanced around, trying to get his bearings as the glow of headlights approached. The two stoops between which he had secreted himself were situated firmly in the middle of the block; there was no way of reaching the next street without being seen. Terrified, he curled himself into a tight bundle in the corner of his hiding place, hoping against hope that the bikers would ride on by.

No such luck. The entire gang roared to a stop almost directly in front of him, forming a large circle facing inward.

Zac recognized the biker-king as he dismounted and moved into the center of the circle, carrying with him a round cage filled with ping-pong balls. He set the cage down in the center of the circle, and spun the balls around and around. All of the bikers watched with rapt attention, clapping their hands in a steady rhythm.

Finally the clapping stopped, and the biker-king reached into the cage and pulled out a single ball. He held it high, and everyone's eyes followed it. Then he lowered it to eye level, and began to laugh.

"What's so funny?" one of the men asked. "Who's the Chosen One?"

The biker-king continued to laugh and tossed the ball high in the air, deftly catching it as it came down. "The name on the ball is mine."

There was a collective gasp from the gathered men, and they all seemed to lean in closer.

"You have to choose a successor," a voice called from the crowd.

"A successor? Gentlemen, gentlemen, I am not the fool our dear departed Larry was. My proxy will not escape."

"Are you so sure you will find a proxy?"

The biker-king laughed once more, throwing back his head and spreading his arms with his mirth. "Oh so very sure, my friend."

Zac pushed himself harder against the corner. Sweat dripped down his forehead, bathed his underarms, trickled down his back.

The biker-king made a slow, deliberate circle, sniffing at the air, nostrils flaring, eyes closed. When his nose pointed at Zac, he smiled, and his eyes slowly opened.

Zac was pinned. Every instinct in his body urged him to run, and yet there was nowhere to go. The biker-king strode toward him, his men breaking ranks, allowing him to pass outside of the circle.

Scrambling to his feet, Zac lit out, head down, arms pumping, running as hard as he could. His vision blurred, and he could hear nothing. Gasping, wheezing, churning, he ran, ran until something slammed into the back of his knees, pitching him straight forward.

He held out his arms to break his fall, but his head smacked the pavement anyway, and with a surge of pain, he blacked out.

Guiltily, Cecile put down the phone. They would find a substitute to teach her classes today. They had done it before for innumerable teachers, and surely not *all* of them had been genuinely sick. She pulled her bathrobe tighter around her and tucked her feet back under the covers.

There was a soft knock on the door; then Bess stepped in without waiting to be invited. She looked at Cecile, still dressed in her nightgown and robe, and raised an eyebrow.

"You'll be late for work," she said. She knew, of course, that Cecile was aware of that; the only reason for the statement was to try to pry more information out of her. Last night, Cecile had explained little about what had happened to Zac, only that he was in the hospital, and that it was serious. It was one of the few times ever Cecile had managed to ward off Bess's insistent questions. Now the siege was to begin again.

"So will you, if you don't hurry," Cecile said, standing up. Bess took a couple more steps into the room. "Bess, go to work. Please."

"What kind of friend would leave you all alone in the state

you're in? If you called in sick, I can too. We'll have a day just for us girls."

Cecile looked her straight in the eye. "No, Bess. We won't. You'd show your friendship for me best by just leaving me alone and going to work. For once, listen to what I'm saying. I want you to leave. Do you understand?" She continued to meet Bess's gaze, and noticed for the first time a hint of uncertainty.

"I understand that's what you want," Bess said slowly. "I'm just not sure that's what you need."

Just for an instant, Cecile tried to control herself. Then all the anger and frustration and hurt burst out of her in a savage howl. "Goddamn it, Bess! Leave me the hell alone!" She gave Bess a shove out of her bedroom, then slammed the door so loud she rattled the perfume bottles on her bureau. Hands shaking, she locked the door and flung herself onto her bed, covering her ears with her hands so she wouldn't hear Bess pounding on the door or shouting soothing platitudes.

In time, the rage faded, and Cecile uncovered her ears and sat up. All was quiet, save for the soft whimpering of Pantagruel who had parked himself outside the door as usual. Cautiously, Cecile walked to the door and opened it a crack. Panta shot in and began a bouncing, running dance of joy around her legs. Bess was nowhere to be seen.

Cecile tried to savor having gotten the upper hand with Bess for once, but could not. Disgusted with herself, she wandered into the kitchen. Bess had made coffee, and Cecile poured herself a cup. She took a sip, grimaced, then took another long gulp. She would drink the too-strong coffee, because it was the only way she could apologize to Bess at this moment.

She cried softly, and when Panta reared up and tentatively licked her hand, she sank to the floor, taking the dog into her lap, stroking the soft fur on his head. He was the only friend left to her, and she hugged him tightly until he whimpered and squirmed.

The first thing Zac noticed was the vicious pain in his head; the next, that his shoulders were aching. With a groan, he opened his eyes.

He was sitting alone near an all-too-familiar street. The mouth of the parking deck yawned before him, as menacing as ever. He struggled, trying to stand, but he was weak, and his hands were cuffed behind him. He sank back to the ground and bowed his head, steeling himself for the ordeal to come.

Ariadne had said that in the previous level of the labyrinth, he could not be harmed. Could that be true of this level also? The throbbing of his head, where it had hit the pavement, told him the answer. Barring a miracle, he was about to die.

A long, thin wail emanated from the parking deck.

Not yet! He wasn't ready! He found the strength to rise to his feet. He shut his eyes tightly. If only he could wake up now, as he had when the Minotaur was almost upon him.

The wailing grew louder, closer, the sound filling his ears. He shook his head, unwilling to face his fate. A hand touched his thigh. He jerked away and kicked out, trying to struggle even as he prayed he would awaken. Quickly, the hand was back, stroking him, moving slowly inward, and Zac opened his eyes.

Ariadne laughed and laughed as Zac's jaw dropped in surprise. She continued to stroke the inside of his thigh as she pursed her lips and imitated the bleak wail of the wraiths. Zac jerked from her touch, but she stayed close, kept her hand between his thighs.

"There, there, Hamlet. Would you rather have the wraiths

touch you there? Or there?" Zac sucked in a quick breath. "Oh, you like that, do you?" she murmured.

"No!" Zac said, but his voice was choked, and her hand was on the evidence. "Let me go," he begged.

"Now that's an interesting request. Are you asking me to let go, or are you asking me to take those handcuffs off of you?"

She deftly opened his jeans and wormed her hand inside. "Please!" he said, humiliated that she could arouse him like this.

"All right," she said, still stroking him. "I'll set you free as long as you meet two simple conditions."

"Anything!"

"First, you continue on into the parking deck."

"But the wraiths!"

"If you don't make this take too long, they won't be there yet." She rubbed harder, squeezing rhythmically. Zac tried again to pull away, but she squeezed even harder. "You're in rather a vulnerable position right now, dear," she said. "I wouldn't move if I were you."

"Stop it."

"Don't you want to know my second condition?"

"What is it?"

She moved closer to him, pressing her breasts against him and raising her lips almost to his. "When you get to the next level of the labyrinth," she murmured hotly, "you'll stop fighting me."

She stroked harder, and Zac couldn't think straight. The intense desire would not go away.

"Think about it before you say no, Hamlet. Those wraiths will come eventually. I can leave you here and watch them slowly eat you alive."

"You won't. You need me to fight Carcajou!" Her touch

was too much for him, and he could feel climax approaching.

"Don't fool yourself. I'm in a much stronger bargaining position than you are."

"All right, all right!" Zac sobbed, knowing as he said the words that she couldn't force him to keep this promise.

She abruptly removed her hand from his pants. He closed his eyes and breathed deeply, trying to calm the racing of his pulse and the shortness of his breath. He felt her move behind him, then felt her hands on his wrists, groping for the lock on the handcuffs. In a moment, he heard the soft snick of the cuffs coming open.

"Just think what the future holds," Ariadne said.

Zac stared toward the parking deck. It was the last place in the world he wanted to go.

Refusing to look at Ariadne again, he started toward the doorway to the next level.

Cecile glanced at her watch. It was 5:00. She was still wearing her robe and slippers; somehow, it had been too much trouble to dress. Her stomach rumbled. She hadn't eaten anything except an overripe apple all day, and there was nothing in the fridge. If she wanted anything substantial to eat, she would have to go to the grocery store.

Twenty minutes later, she stood before the door, strangely reluctant to open it. Could she face interacting with people? What if she missed a call from George while she was at the store? She sighed, as her stomach rumbled again. She would have to leave the apartment once in a while, so she might as well get used to it now. She opened the door.

On the doorstep lay a single, blood-red rosebud with an envelope beneath it. She picked up the rose and held it to her nose. It was sweet and fragrant. She opened the envelope, knowing instinctively who it would be from.

Inside was a card with a reproduction of a soft, pastel flower garden, filled primarily with red roses. Opening the card, Cecile beheld an angular and yet graceful and precise script.

My dear Cecile,

The light of day often makes clear what was murky the night before. This day's light has shown me what an ass I was last night. In trying to be suave and impress you, I've succeeded only in chasing you away. Please accept this rose as a token of my apology.

If you would deign to speak to me again after my insufferable behavior, I would appreciate another chance. I don't want to lose your friendship through my clumsy advances.

Once again, I ask your forgiveness.

Yours,

Carl

Cecile stepped back inside. She put Carl's card down and went to the kitchen to get a vase for the rose. What should she make of *this* development?

Certainly his card was more eloquent and appealing than anything he had said to her in person. Had he decided to try another tack? Or was the card sincere? Or, had Bess run into him this morning and given him a piece of her mind for cornering Cecile last night?

The least likely possibility was sincerity. If only Carl *could* be a friend to her. She was sorely in need of one.

The phone rang, and Cecile's heart went thud in her chest. Could it be George?

Her mouth gone dry and her hands shaking, she picked up the receiver. "Hello?" There was a long pause in which she heard only the crackle of static. Then, a hissed intake of breath.

"Have you forgotten me, Precious?" a slithery voice asked.

"I surely have not forgotten you."

Cecile let out a muffled scream and slammed down the phone. "Oh my God, no!" she cried. She knew that voice! It was indelibly burned in her memory, as was his face, as was the alcohol-and-lust smell of him. Her skin shuddered with the memory of his hands roughly touching her breasts and her thighs. She was not imagining things, she was not being paranoid. He was out there. Why, after all this time?

"Oh, Zac. Please, please wake up. I need you so badly." She wrapped her arms around herself.

How long would he toy with her before he pounced? He had known her phone number, and her number was unlisted. And he knew where she worked. He could be outside her door even now.

What was she to do? The police? She could call the police! But no threat had been made; what could *they* do? She knew the answer to that. Steve did too.

Snatching up her purse, she strode purposefully to the door and yanked it open. If she couldn't control what Steve did, she *could* control how she reacted to it. How he would enjoy it if she became so fearful of him that she wouldn't even leave her apartment to buy groceries! She would not give him that satisfaction.

Stepping outside, she halted abruptly as she saw Carl ascending the stairs. His eyes fastened on her instantly. For once, he didn't have a lascivious smile. Instead, he looked down and scuffed his shoe.

"Hi," he said.

"Hi," she replied, guarded.

"I guess you got my little token of apology."

"Yes."

"Let me add one in person. I'm afraid I'd had a little too much to drink last night. I woke up this morning with a headache, feeling really stupid."

He hadn't seemed drunk last night. Certainly he hadn't behaved any differently than any other time she had been with him.

"I know what you're thinking," he said. "You're thinking I acted just like I always act."

Cecile started, but he didn't seem to notice.

"Cecile, I'm really not like that." He still didn't look at her, and the late afternoon sun cast a shadow over his face, hiding his eyes. He scratched the back of his head, suddenly seeming as lost and vulnerable as . . . Zac. "Believe it or not, I'm actually kind of shy."

Cecile rolled her eyes and almost laughed.

"Well, I used to be. I had to fight with myself to talk to people. I hated it. Then I discovered that if I acted like I had self-confidence coming out my ears, people tended to like me. Women, anyway." His cheeks turned a soft pink. "Now, it seems, I don't have the good sense to turn it off when I see that it's turning someone else off."

He met her eyes for the first time. She felt the familiar surge in her pulse though it wasn't so alarming this time, maybe because of its very familiarity. He sounded and looked sincere. Still . . .

Cecile thought of the phone call she'd just received, the voice she had been dreading to hear for so long. All well and good to tell herself that she would bravely defy Steve, but that didn't mean she had to make a target of herself. Maybe she *should* give Carl one more chance.

But if she gave him even the slightest hint of encouragement, could she ever shake him?

"I was planning on walking to the grocery store," she said.

"Do you need anything?"

Carl's eyes lit up, and he smiled. "Why, yes. I do seem to be out of some household necessities. Besides, it's a beautiful day for a walk."

She tried to return his smile, but she was sure her nervousness showed through.

"You seem nervous," Carl said. "I mean, even more than usual. Is anything the matter?"

"No," she answered, too quickly.

Carl shrugged. "You don't have to tell me," he said. "I haven't earned your trust yet."

She didn't answer. She wasn't telling *anyone* about Steve. There would be too much explaining, and explaining it was almost like reliving it. She hadn't yet managed to tell Zac, the man she loved.

Zac! She had heard nothing about him all day. She would have to go to the hospital when she got back from the store. If George wasn't going to keep her informed, maybe she could corner a doctor and force *him* to tell her what was going on.

Carl, with a sensitivity Cecile hadn't thought he had, refrained from forcing conversation on her. It was nice, in a way, to walk with him, to have the feeling of not being wholly alone, and yet without having to chatter. She felt safer with him by her side. He was strong. He was capable. Surely Steve wouldn't dare approach her while Carl was with her.

At the store, Cecile half-heartedly chose some frozen dinners. She couldn't face anything that took more work, and she doubted she could get herself to eat much anyway. Carl, who had gone off by himself in the store, was waiting for her behind the checkout when she finished. He had a small paper bag in his hand. "Got everything you need?" he asked.

She nodded.

Silence prevailed again as they made their way back to the apartment building. They entered the parking lot, and saw that Bess's car was there. Cecile sighed softly. The last thing she wanted now was to face Bess. How could she retract the cruel words she had spoken so thoughtlessly this morning? Still, Bess deserved an apology, and the sooner the better.

"Thanks for walking with me," she told Carl. "I'd better get this stuff into the freezer."

"Does your roommate often leave the door open?" Carl asked.

Cecile glanced up. The door *was* ajar. "She knows better than that. Panta could get out."

She started up the stairs, but stopped abruptly. Was it possible Steve was in there? If he knew her phone number, he undoubtedly knew her address. "Bess!" she called out, but got no answer. "Bess!"

Carl passed Cecile on the stairs. "You wait here," he said. "I'll make sure everything's all right."

"I'm sure it is," Cecile said, without conviction, taking another step toward the apartment. Carl held out his hand to stop her, carefully refraining from touching her.

"Please, Cecile. Call me old-fashioned, call me paranoid, whatever. But let me go in there first."

Cecile shifted her groceries from one hip to the other. She wanted to put them down. "Bess!" she called loudly.

Carl scowled, but the expression passed so quickly Cecile wasn't sure she saw it. There was still no answer from the apartment. Surely Bess had heard her.

Reaching the top step, Carl peeked inside the apartment, then cautiously stepped in.

Cecile stood frozen, her spine tingling. Stop this, Cecile, she thought. Bess accidentally left the door open when she took Panta for a walk.

But Bess never took walks, with or without Panta.

Minutes passed, and Carl hadn't reappeared. Something had to be wrong, terribly wrong. Trembling, Cecile took a step upward, just as Carl appeared at the head of the stairs. His face was grim. He came to her and she dropped her bag of groceries.

"God, no," she whispered, covering her mouth with her hand.

Carl reached out and put a hand on her shoulder. "We need to call the police," he said softly.

Cecile shook her head back and forth. "No."

"We can call from my apartment."

"No."

He tried to guide her down the stairs but she shook his arm off and made a dash for her door. Carl grabbed her arm and spun her around with such force that she would have toppled down the stairs had he not caught her.

"Please, Cecile! Don't go in there." Still she struggled against him, but his grip was firm. He grabbed her chin and forced her to look at him. "For once, trust me," he begged. "You don't need to see. Come with me."

She screamed then. Screamed so loud that her neighbors came bolting out of their apartments. Screamed so loud she thought she'd tear her throat out.

6

Water dripped nearby, and somewhere in the depths, an electrical buzz droned incessantly. The solitary light bulb flickered and fizzled and finally popped, flooding the parking deck in blackness.

Zac shivered, the dank building having long since dispelled the intense heat Ariadne had aroused in him. Inching along, his back pressed tightly against a wall, he tried to suppress the memory of Ariadne's hand on him, of the effect that hand had had. No one had ever touched him like that before.

The faint sound of a wail echoed through the structure. The wraiths! He had to find the doorway into the next level of the labyrinth, and before they discovered him. It was somewhere in the deck, he knew, but the feeling of dread that had led him here was now omnidirectional, and he could only guess at which way to go.

The wailing grew more distinct. Groping his way down one wall, up another, wondering what he was looking for, Zac eventually came upon a cold steel door. Was this the way out? He fought down a swell of fear and turned the knob. The door was stuck. He shoved against it with his shoulder, then shoved harder, harder, till it gave way. He stepped through . . .

. . . and was hit with a blast of icy wind so numbingly cold it sucked the air from his lungs. He gasped, and quickly flung his arms around himself. Frigid gusts tore at him like knives, penetrating his clothes, numbing his feet and hands. Wind-whipped pellets of snow bit into his cheeks, his nose, his neck. He had never experienced cold like this; he had to find shelter quickly, or he would die.

It was almost pitch black. Squinting into the darkness, he stepped forward, plowing through thigh-deep snow. His lungs ached sharply, and he had to force them to take in air. Already he felt light-headed; he remembered that he hadn't eaten or drunk in . . . how long? He didn't even know.

Moaning in misery, Zac trudged ahead, muscles straining, head lowered to his chest, knowing he wouldn't get far but knowing if he didn't keep moving he would succumb to the cold even faster. He couldn't feel his feet or his hands at all now, and the numbness was climbing up through his legs. "Ariadne!" he hollered, his voice competing with the fierce howls of the wind. Surely she would know where to find shelter. Where *was* she?

Soon he felt sleepy. Panic surged through him, for he knew what it meant to feel sleepy: it meant his body was giving in to the cold; it meant it wouldn't be long before he collapsed. "Ariadne!" he shouted again and again, but the wind swallowed his voice, and the cold crept down his throat.

Trying to take just one more step, he pitched face-first into the snow, and as he struggled to regain his feet, fatigue seized him, and held him. "Ariadne!" he tried to call, but it came out a whimper.

He closed his eyes and let the cold engulf him.

Cecile sat, dry-eyed, on Carl's black leather sofa. The flash-ing blue and red of the police lights shone through his first-floor window. She could hear the squawking of the police radio, the hushed murmurs of curious neighbors, the heavy tread of the paramedics' feet as they carried Bess's body down the steps and into the ambulance. Carl was out there with them, answering their questions and stubbornly refusing to allow them to talk to her. She didn't know what she could tell them anyway. She hadn't been home when it had happened; she didn't even know *what* had happened. All she knew was that Bess was dead. And that the last words she had spoken to Bess had been the cruelest she'd ever uttered.

Carl slipped in the door. There was still activity outside, but from the sound of closing car doors, Cecile guessed it was beginning to die down. Carl took her hand, and they sat together in silence as tears sprang again to Cecile's eyes and slowly trickled down her cheeks.

"The police will have to take your statement," Carl said quietly.

Cecile started to rise.

"Not now," he stopped her. "I told them you'd been hysterical, and had taken some tranquilizers, and convinced them it could wait until tomorrow."

"You *convinced* them? The police?"

"My powers of persuasion are legendary—even if they don't work on you." He smiled. "Still, I think it's best you go first thing in the morning. I'll go with you, of course."

She hesitated, then nodded. She couldn't, just couldn't, face this alone. She waited until she was sure she could speak without her voice cracking, and asked, "What happened?"

Carl tightened his grip on her hand. "It looks like Bess killed herself, sweetheart."

"What?" Cecile surged to her feet, tearing her hand out of Carl's. She had been fully prepared to hear that Bess had been murdered. She even knew who had done it; knew who had counted on Cecile being too frightened by his phone call to go out; knew who had come to the apartment looking for her.

And had found Bess there instead.

But that wasn't what Carl had just said, was it? He had said . . .

"That's impossible!"

Carl stood up and reached for her hand again. She twitched away from him. "I know it sounds impossible," he said. "but there's really no question."

She shook her head violently. "I will *never* believe that Bess killed herself! She was murdered!"

"Cecile—"

"Bess was much too . . . too strong-willed! And she was happy. She loved her life, and everything always went right for her."

"Maybe she wasn't as strong as you thought."

"She was! She was the strongest person I ever knew!"

"All right. Don't get angry. I only meant that on the inside she may have been more fragile than she seemed, and when something finally went wrong for her, something you might not even know about, she couldn't handle it."

"No!" Cecile insisted, but her mind traveled back to this morning, to angry words spoken in haste. But that was ridiculous! No words of Cecile's had ever before scratched the surface of Bess's confidence. Bess was murdered, and the murderer had made it look like suicide.

Steve was being careful. He didn't want the police involved, so he left notes that only hinted at menace, made phone calls with no overt threat. And killed Cecile's friend without revealing that he even existed.

"She was murdered, Carl."

"Cecile, I saw her. She had slit her wrists all the way up to her elbows, then let herself bleed into the sink until she was too weak to stand."

"No!"

"And there was a note."

"A note?"

"Yes. It was on the table."

"A note," she repeated dully. "What did it say?"

Carl, uncharacteristically, hesitated. Cecile looked up at him and saw uncertainty in his eyes. It was an expression he wore awkwardly. "I'm sure the police will show it to you in the morning." Even his voice sounded unsure, and he averted his eyes.

"What did it say?"

He shook his head. "You've had enough today. Just let it lie. There'll be time for everything in the morning. For now, let me make you a nice cup of tea. And maybe you should take a sleeping pill. I have some."

"What did it say?" she repeated, as if he hadn't spoken.

Carl let out a deep sigh and sat down on the sofa, patting the seat beside him. Cecile stared at him. He crossed his legs and leaned back into the sofa, and she realized he would not tell her unless she sat beside him. Stiffly, she complied. Carl sat up straighter and took her hand once more. She didn't have the strength to pull away again.

"It said, *You wanted me to leave you alone. I hope you're happy*." His voice was low and soothing as he tried to soften the blow, but Cecile felt like she'd been punched in the gut. Her vision swam, her ears rang. It couldn't be. It just couldn't be!

There had to be a rational explanation for that note. Cecile's words wouldn't have driven Bess to suicide, and even if they had, Bess wasn't spiteful enough to strike back from the grave like that. This was nonsense!

"Steve murdered her," she declared. "He was stalking me this morning. Obviously he overheard our argument, and decided to use it to hurt me." Her face flushed, and she felt so giddy with relief at the explanation that she almost laughed.

Carl frowned deeply. "Cecile, honey, what are you talking about? Who's Steve?"

"It's a long story," she told him. "But he killed Bess, I'm sure of it. And he wrote that note to try to make it look like suicide, so no one would suspect him."

"I see," Carl said carefully, watching her as if he expected her to start foaming at the mouth at any moment.

"I know I sound paranoid. But even if Bess did decide to kill herself, she wouldn't have opened the front door first. Someone left that door open. When the police check the handwriting on the note and see it's not Bess's, they'll go after Steve and they'll catch him. And I'll be safe."

"*You'll* be safe? So Steve is after you, too?"

"I'm the *only* one he's after. Don't you see? It's my fault Bess is dead."

Carl started to say something, then changed his mind. "I'll get you that cup of tea now."

It was clear that Carl thought she was babbling—a woman driven to hysterics by tragic events as yet too raw to put aside. He hadn't believed a word she'd said. And neither would the police. The police would *want* to think that Bess killed herself. It was the tidiest, easiest solution.

Steve was counting on her not being believed. Just as he had so long ago, when she had caught him with his girlfriend and he had just grinned at her and pumped a little faster.

Bess hadn't believed that Steve was back after all these years. Had there been a moment when he was in the apartment and Bess had realized who he was? She must have been terrified! And what had Steve done to her? Had he knocked her unconscious and then slit her wrists? Threatened her with torture and rape if she didn't kill herself? It *must* have been something like that.

Carl returned to the sofa and handed her a steaming cup of tea. She drank a few sips. Maybe she should rehearse what she was going to say to the police. If she could convince Carl, it would give her more confidence tomorrow.

"Carl—" she began.

"Shh," he said. "Drink your tea first. It will help calm your nerves. Then we'll talk."

Calm her nerves indeed! What he meant was bring her back to her senses! "I'm not hysterical, Carl. Or hadn't you noticed?"

"I did notice. But the tea might relax you anyway. Go ahead."

Fuming, she drank more tea, and Carl nodded approvingly. She glared at him and put the cup to her lips, downing the rest of the contents. That was when she noticed the bitter aftertaste in her mouth. Alarmed, she looked at him.

He smiled sheepishly. "I put a sleeping pill in your tea," he admitted. "I was afraid in the state you were in you might refuse to take one, and the sleep will do you good."

"Bastard!" she cried, standing up. Already she felt woozy, and her knees almost buckled. She staggered, and Carl sprang to his feet to steady her. "What did you give me?"

"Something strong," he replied as her legs gave out completely and he scooped her into his arms.

Something hot and bitter forced its way into Zac's mouth and slithered down his throat. He gagged, coughing and fighting for air. The bitter taste lingered in his mouth and a bolt of heat burned its way toward his stomach.

When he finally stopped coughing, he looked around. He

was in a one-room cabin, lying on the floor near the hearth, covered in a heavy, fur-lined skin that smelled like it hadn't been cured properly. A wood fire blazed in the fireplace, a little closer than was comfortable. Outside the cabin, the wind screamed.

Ariadne, wearing the same cloak she always wore, was squatting beside him, holding a vial filled with steaming fluid. "I take it you don't like my little cure-all," she said, bolting down the remains of the vial in one gulp. Sensuously, she licked her lips to get the last drops. "It's good for you. Gives you lots of energy—especially when you haven't eaten anything for days."

She went to the hearth and filled the vial once more from a small black kettle. The viscous, amber fluid steamed as she held the vial out to Zac. "Drink!"

The awful taste was still in his mouth from the last sip.

"You'd rather die of starvation?" she said.

However repulsive the stuff might be, Zac had to drink it. He tried to reach for the vial, but his arm refused to move, and he realized he could feel neither his feet nor his hands. He tried to shrug the fur off of him, but his shoulders responded sluggishly and the fur slid down only a few inches. He noticed then that he was naked, and the blood rose to his face.

"Your clothes were soaked through," Ariadne told him. "Come now, drink your medicine like a good little boy."

"I can't," he said, barely managing a whisper.

Ariadne feigned surprise. "Oh! That's right. I forgot about the frostbite! I'm afraid your arms and legs have had it. And your ears and nose too." She pulled down the fur to show him his arms. They were a ghastly, bloodless white. "They'll get more colorful when the gangrene sets in," she said, grinning at him.

Zac's throat closed up with panic. Was he truly going to rot away, slowly, while she sat beside him and gloated?

"Relax, Hamlet, dear," she cooed. "I'll take good care of you. You're not too likely to defeat Carcajou without your arms and legs." She poured some of the amber fluid onto her left hand, then put the vial down and spread the fluid over both her hands. "This is going to hurt," she warned, rubbing the medicine into his lifeless right arm. "In the world you know, the doctors would be helpless to do anything but amputate when it's gone this far. Here, there is a cure."

His arm started to tingle. She was telling the truth! She *could* cure him! The liquid burned into his arm, as it had burned its way down his throat. His eyes teared, and he gritted his teeth, willing himself to bear the pain without complaint.

"That ought to do it," Ariadne said. She poured more liquid on her hands and began to minister to his other arm. The pain from his right arm was subsiding as his left began to tingle. He grabbed the edge of the fur with his now healthy right hand and clung to it.

Finished with his arms, Ariadne rubbed the healing fluid on his ears and nose. He closed his eyes to better bear the pain, and waited for her to begin on his feet and legs, waited apprehensively for the fierce tingling to begin.

Nothing. He opened his eyes. Ariadne had rocked back on her heels and was watching him with a thoughtful expression on her face.

"Why'd you stop?" he asked, though he was sure he wouldn't like the answer.

"I had a thought," she said. "It occurred to me that there's another part of your body that needs massaging." She reached out suddenly and yanked the fur completely away from him. He yelped and sat up quickly, reaching for the fur, but she flung it across the room, and he was left naked before her. As usual in her presence, he had a humiliating erection. "I didn't *think* the frostbite had gone up that far," she said, her mischievous smile slowly fading into something softer. She reached out and touched his cheek with her velvet-soft fingers.

Zac shook his head. "Why? Why would you want a man like me, anyway? And why like this?"

"I have many secrets," she murmured, her face moving closer and closer to him. "I'm afraid this is one I cannot share with you."

"First cure my legs!" he said, but he was only begging for time, and she knew it.

"You're much more likely to keep your promise to me if I wait awhile to cure your legs."

"What promise?!"

"Your promise not to fight me."

He had almost allowed himself to forget about the shameful promise he had made to save himself from the wraiths! How right she was to assume he would try to break it.

"I'll keep it," he said, trying to sound convincing.

She shook her head. "No, I don't think you will. Now is the time, Hamlet. You've tried to hedge your bets just like your hero. It worked out badly for him, and I'm afraid it won't work out any better for you."

"But I can't do it without my legs!"

She laughed. "My, how unimaginative." Her hand began the rhythmic stroking he could not resist, and fire surged through his veins. Her skin had a faint, musky smell that filled his senses, and as the tip of her tongue darted out and barely touched his lower lip, his mouth opened, almost against his will. Suddenly her body was against his, her lips and tongue filling his mouth.

His hands tore away her cloak and his fingers found her full, firm breasts. He couldn't take his hands from her perfect body. She leaned into his hands, moaning softly. Then, she straddled him and slowly lowered herself onto him.

His ears roared and he could see nothing, smell nothing, feel nothing but her, as she moved, expertly, on top of him. He closed his eyes and threw back his head, mouth open. Ariadne moved faster, her breath coming in short, moaning gasps. Zac wanted this to last forever, wanted to lose himself in the reckless, mindless, animal pleasure. But that was impossible and, after what seemed like only moments, he came, his rapture so great that he screamed.

When it was over, even before the surge of adrenaline had ended, the realization of what he had done came crashing down on Zac. He had betrayed Cecile! His heart still pounding, he heaved Ariadne off of him, ignoring her startled bleat, and turned his back to her, and cried.

"You know, Hamlet dear," she said, still breathless, "It's generally the girl who's supposed to cry when she loses her virginity, not the boy!"

"Shut up!" He almost turned to her, wanting more than anything to lash out at her with his fists. But that would mean looking at her, and he couldn't bear that.

He had been so sure he could resist her. Yes, she had forced the action, but in the end, he had surrendered not to her extortion, but to the intoxicating feel of her body against his.

He had not protested enough.

"Racked with guilt so quickly?" Ariadne murmured. "Poor thing. It was my impression that you didn't think this world real. If it's not real, then why so remorseful?"

"It's real enough."

She settled herself beside him, pressing close. Her fingers

toyed absently with the hair on his chest, and her lips brushed his shoulder. "Don't feel too bad," she whispered. "Cecile won't last much longer than you. Then, you can feel guilty together."

"You're wrong. You don't know Cecile."

"Is she so much stronger than you, then?"

Zac ignored the mockery in her voice. Cecile *is* stronger, he thought. "You got what you wanted," he told Ariadne. "Now, heal my legs."

"All in good time, my dear," she said, fingers sliding down his chest. "All in good time."

Cecile awoke, warm and cozy. Zac's body was pressed up against her back, his knees nestled behind hers, his arm protectively around her shoulders. He was snoring softly. She snuggled a little closer to him. His snoring faltered a moment, and he held her a little tighter, his hand shifting downward to her breast. Then the snores resumed.

She yawned. The alarm wasn't sounding yet; she wondered how long she had. Come to think of it, had she set the alarm last night? Was this a school day, or a weekend? It must be a weekend; Zac wouldn't be with her on a weekday morning. Her head felt full of cobwebs. Why couldn't she remember what day of the week it was? She opened her eyes.

She was in an unfamiliar room. A small bronze figurine of a well-endowed naked woman stood atop a dark, masculine dresser, across from the bed. Sunlight streamed in through the gap between dark red curtains. The snoring continued beside her, and Cecile realized with a start that this was *not* Zac.

The memory of last night came flooding back. Bess was dead! And this was Carl's apartment! She remembered, vaguely, that he had put something in her tea. Sweat popped

out all over her body. She lifted the cover carefully, so as not
to wake Carl. His hand was cupped around her breast, but
she was still wearing her bra and panties. Surely, he hadn't
taken advantage of her drugged state last night! She grabbed
him by the wrist, gingerly, and nudged his hand away from
her breast.

Carl woke and jerked his hand away. He sat up, running
a hand through his hair and looking very sheepish. "Jesus,
Cecile," he said. "I'm sorry! I didn't mean to get fresh with
you." He subtly moved his body away from hers. "How are
you feeling?"

"Groggy," was all she could think to reply.

"That'll fade. I hope you'll forgive me for taking things
into my own hands." He heard the double entendre in his
words and grinned apologetically. "I really thought you needed sleep, and I wasn't about to take you back to your apartment."

"You could have left me on the sofa."

The rakish grin was back on his face. "My willpower's not
that strong. But don't worry: I didn't ravish you in your
sleep."

Cecile blushed. "I didn't mean to imply—"

"I know. I didn't take it as an accusation."

He propped his head on his hand and looked at her, the
covers artfully draped over his hips. She couldn't help but
notice the firm, muscular lines of his arms and chest, and the
way his hair, loose from its ponytail and tossed about by
sleep, framed his face and shoulders. A part of her wanted to
reach out and touch it. She felt the color rise to her cheeks,
and quickly averted her eyes.

"I have to get back to my apartment," she said, sitting up.
She hadn't called the hospital, or George, or been anywhere
that they could reach her.

There was an antique, straight-backed chair in the far corner of the room, and Cecile'sr clothes were neatly folded over the back of it. She threw the covers off and got to her feet, acutely aware that Carl was watching her, but also aware that he could have stared at her for hours on end last night when he had taken her clothes off. She took one step toward the chair, then abruptly sat back down as a wave of nausea struck her.

"Whoa, take it easy there, honey," Carl said. "That pill I gave you was pretty strong stuff. Give yourself a little time."

"No, I have to go home. I have to check my answering machine. And my dog! Oh, God," she groaned. "I forgot about poor Panta!"

Carl shook his head. "The dog wasn't in the apartment. It must have gotten out."

"Oh," she said. Had Panta really gotten out, or had Steve taken him?

Carl slid out of the bed and stretched. He was wearing the bottoms only of a pair of silk pajamas. The silk fluttered sensuously with his movements as he retrieved her clothes from the chair and brought them to her. He sat beside her on the bed, a fraction of an inch closer than was comfortable, and she noticed a faint, spicy scent to him, as if he had splashed on some aftershave about an hour or so ago. But he had been asleep, so that had to be her imagination.

"Perhaps your dog—Panta did you say her name was?"

"*His* name. Yes, short for Pantagruel."

Carl laughed. "Big name for such a little dog. But I like it. Anyway, maybe we should put some fliers up in the neighborhood. Surely he wouldn't wander too far."

That might work if Panta had actually run away, she thought.

"I have to go home anyway," she said. "My boyfriend is in

the hospital, and his brother's going to call to let me know how he's doing. I have to check my answering machine."

"Ah! I was wondering why you didn't call him yesterday. Listen, can I make a suggestion?"

She looked at him warily.

"Let *me* go to your apartment. I'll check your messages. I mean, do you *really* want to go in there now?"

"It's not a haunted house!" she said tartly, but she wondered, could she step into the bathroom where Bess had died, without visualizing what must have happened there? Could she step into her own bedroom, without remembering the woman-to-woman talks they'd had there? Without looking at the door she had only yesterday slammed in Bess's face? Tears sprang to her eyes.

"I can pack you a suitcase, and you can stay with me if you like," he said gently. "I'll sleep on the sofa, if you prefer."

He looked sincere enough. Still, she couldn't imagine spending another night in his apartment, even if he did sleep on the couch. Her skin crawled at the thought of how helpless she had been before him last night. Maybe he hadn't "ravished her in her sleep," as he put it; but that didn't mean he wouldn't in the future. "It's very kind of you to offer, Carl. Don't think I don't appreciate the thought. But I can't accept. It would just be too awkward."

"Is there somewhere else you can go?" he asked, looking hurt. "Somewhere where you won't be alone? Your parents, maybe?"

Cecile shook her head. "My mother lives in California." She could hardly fly off to California now! Zac needed her. "I guess I'll stay at Zac's."

"By yourself? When you think some madman murdered your roommate and is after you?"

"*You* don't believe that."

He shrugged. "What matters is what *you* believe. And what the police believe."

"I suppose that's true," she conceded. "And when they find that the note isn't in Bess's handwriting, they'll believe me."

But what if the note *is* in Bess's handwriting? she thought. If Steve threatened her with something so dire that she would rather slit her wrists than endure it, surely that threat could have compelled her to write the note. Then the police would ignore Cecile's cries of "murder," and Steve would be free to kill again.

And she knew who was next.

"Well, if you change your mind, let me know," Carl said. "You can call me any time, and I'll come get you." He grabbed a slip of paper and scribbled a phone number. "This is my cell phone number," he said, handing her the paper.

She nodded. For once, Carl wasn't smiling. His eyes looked troubled, as if he were truly worried about her. It was some comfort to know that there was still someone she could go to as a last resort.

"Tell you what," Carl said. "I'll make you a cup of tea—unspiked. You can drink it while I'm getting your clothes and things. Then, we'll go to the police station together. I'll drop you off at Zac's afterwards."

"I'll need my car," she said.

He slapped his hand against his forehead dramatically. "What an idiot!" he said. "All right, I guess I'll bring you back here to get your car. Is that a plan?"

She nodded. "But when you go to my apartment, there's something else I need you to get for me. There's a note, sitting on the nightstand beside my bed. It's from the man who killed Bess. I have to show it to the police."

"I'll get it," he said as he rummaged through his dresser and pulled out some briefs, black jeans, and a white t-shirt.

He turned his back to her and let his pajamas drop. Cecile's face flamed. He was naked. Her heartbeat elevated a notch, even as she tactfully looked away.

Carl pulled his clothes on, apparently unaware that his nakedness had in any way affected her. His hair still loose around his shoulders, he headed for the door. "I'll bring your tea in a moment," he said.

"Make it coffee."

He turned to her and raised an eyebrow, then laughed and shook his head.

Zac sat up and looked around him. The fire had died down, and a chill pervaded the room. Ariadne lay sleeping beside him, her lips slightly parted. Her hair shone red in the firelight, and her cheeks were suffused with an artificial blush. Zac carefully pulled back the fur and gazed upon her naked, flawless body. She was the sexiest woman he had ever known, and last night she had proven it time and again. It would have taken an inhuman willpower to rebuff her. Even now, sore and tired as he was, he wanted her.

She moaned softly and turned over, exposing her breasts. So beautiful.

Would his first time have been so good with Cecile? He knew the answer. He remembered what it had felt like to touch Cecile, how her body had stiffened, how her tension had traveled through his fingers and into his body. How difficult, how traumatic that first time would have been for them, with him so uncertain and her so afraid. At least now, when the time came for them to make love, he would have some experience, some idea what to do.

The rationalization fell flat. What had helped Cecile overcome her aversion to being touched had *been* his own uncertainty. It had comforted her, made her feel less threatened, let her trust him. How would she feel now? Would she sense that something had changed in him?

"Still feeling those morning-after regrets?" Ariadne asked.

He hadn't noticed that she'd awakened. He said, "I'll feel them forever."

"But you'll get used to it."

Something about those words sounded harsh and accusatory in his ears. "Yes, I'll get used to it." A wave of vertigo passed through him. He covered his eyes with one hand and grabbed onto Ariadne with the other.

"Don't get your hopes up," she said. "You're much too deep in the labyrinth now."

The vertigo passed, then hit again, worse. Zac's stomach churned, and he felt as if he might throw up, but he was no closer to waking. "What's happening?" he gasped.

"Oh, I'd guess someone in your world is trying very hard to awaken you. A level ago, it might have worked. Now, it's too late."

Someone was trying to wake him up! That meant someone—Cecile?—had found him where he lay senseless in his apartment. He was probably in the hospital by now, tubes protruding from his body, surrounded by university doctors eager to solve his case and make a name for themselves. They were undoubtedly pumping him full of experimental drugs, wondering if one of them would miraculously bring him back.

"How long have I been gone?" he mused aloud.

"Not too long," Ariadne answered. "Your perception of time is substantially altered here. I'd say you've only been out of it for a day or two."

A day or two? It felt like weeks! "I guess that's good news," he said. "It means Carcajou has only had one or two days to work on Cecile."

"That's true. Your lady love is still pure. Unlike you."

Zac glared at her. "Do you know that for a fact?"

"Yes."

"How?"

She just smiled her most insolent smile.

"What happens next?" he asked.

"If you're strong enough, you continue on to the next level of the labyrinth."

"How many levels are there?"

"That's not as easy an answer as you might think. All I can tell you is that you're close to the center. Be stout of heart, Hamlet; it's going to get worse."

"Stop calling me that!"

"Every woman likes to have a pet name for her lover."

"You *could* choose the name of someone who didn't die tragically!"

Ariadne's face turned suddenly cold and hard. "That's all you worry about, isn't it? Your tragic fate. You are more like Hamlet than you know, letting others around you suffer, as long as it suits your purpose."

"What do you mean?" Zac was taken aback by her outburst. "I came deeper into this hell to save Cecile from Carcajou! You told me I had no other choice! I wanted to turn back, if you remember."

"To save Cecile," she mimicked, sneering at him. "What a sanctimonious prick you are! You're not trying to *save* Cecile. You're trying to save her for yourself. There's a difference."

Zac bristled. "That's a cruel and unfair thing to say."

"Admit it. Once Carcajou's had her, you won't want her anymore."

Rage like he'd never known surged through Zac, and he lashed out with his fist, catching Ariadne on the cheek. She grunted, and her head jerked sharply with the force of his blow, but she didn't cry out.

Zac stared, shocked, as a spot of blood welled up at the corner of her mouth. His knuckles smarted where they had hit bone, and he tucked his hand under his arm. He looked down at the floor, breathing hard.

What was he becoming?

Ariadne touched his shoulder softly. "You've taken another small step closer to the center," she said. "To get there, you must know yourself completely, the meanest, basest parts of you, the parts you don't want to know. But if you don't know them, you can never face Carcajou down. It's vital, and I'm going to help you. No matter how much it hurts."

"I hate you," he said, his petulant words sounding thin and hollow.

"I know," she answered. "And that's a step in the right direction."

Zac lowered his head and closed his eyes. Why was she arousing his desires, then mocking and tormenting him at every opportunity? Surely there was purpose to it. But it would do no good to ask her. She told him only what she wanted to tell, and when it suited her.

Ariadne put on her cloak and brushed her hair. She looked beautiful, and strangely unobtainable, though he had had her so many times last night. "It's time to go, Hamlet," she said, a distinct touch of frost in her voice.

"Where?" he asked.

"To the undiscovered country."

"What's *that* supposed to mean?"

"Surely Hamlet knows what the 'undiscovered country' is!"

He met her eyes. "Death. The undiscovered country is death." Strangely, he felt no fear. Perhaps the rigors of his trials had desensitized him. Or perhaps this was just a momentary lapse in his sanity, a numbness brought on by an excess of emotion only recently spent.

"Yes. To reach the next level, you must pass through this country. You must travel there of your own free will, then contrive not to linger."

Zac pushed the heavy fur off of him and walked, naked, to where his clothes were hanging by the fire. "So, how do I get there?" he asked as he dressed, still too numb to be afraid.

"I'll show you the way."

Cecile sat on a hard wooden bench while the police interviewed Carl for the second time. They seemed more interested in what he had to say, as he had found the body, than in listening to her accusations.

As she had feared, when they had shown her the note, she had instantly recognized Bess's handwriting. The words shot daggers into her heart, though she knew they were not Bess's own. Having seen that handwriting, having been forced to explain about the argument, Cecile had been tempted not to tell the police her theory, knowing now that she would not be believed.

To their credit, the officers had listened attentively. They had taken the note from Steve and had promised they would look into his whereabouts and activities. They had asked just the right questions, and had refrained from giving each other any significant looks. Still, Cecile felt sure they were asking just to be thorough, not because they believed Bess might have been murdered.

She crossed her legs and sighed. Why were they taking so long with Carl?

There had been no messages on her answering machine—apparently George didn't think it was any of her business how Zac was doing—so Cecile had telephoned the hospital and spoken to someone in the intensive care unit. Zac's condition was unchanged. That was all she'd been able to learn, and that grudgingly, as she wasn't listed as next of kin.

Carl finally emerged, shaking hands with one of the detectives before coming over to Cecile and extending his elbow.

"Let's get out of this place," he said.

Was it Cecile's imagination, or did the detective—Robbins, if she remembered the name right—studiously avoid looking at her?

"What were they asking you about that took so long?" she asked, standing up and taking his elbow almost by instinct. "I'd have thought they'd asked you enough questions yesterday."

"They asked every single one of them again today. I think that's standard police practice, to make sure I didn't suddenly remember something vital that I failed to mention the last time."

"Did they ask you about me?"

"About you?"

"Did they ask you if I had a history of insanity or paranoia?"

Carl laughed. "No, they just asked about last night."

"Carl," she said, stopping and forcing him to stop as well. She looked into his eyes, bracing herself for the burst of adrenaline that always coursed through her when she did so. "You would tell me if they had asked something like that, wouldn't you? I have to know whether they're taking me seriously or not. I couldn't tell when they were interviewing me."

"I promise, I would tell you. They asked me what my relationship with you was, and I told them you were a friend, and that we hadn't known each other very long. I don't know if they would have asked different questions if I had given a different answer."

He seemed to be leaning in to her, his eyes solid black with hints of silver light burning behind them. Cecile blinked, and the strange light quickly faded.

"Thank you," she said, but she was hit with an urge to disentangle her arm from his. What was it about him that made her so uneasy, and yet so wildly attracted to him at the same time?

"So," Carl said, guiding her through the halls of the police station toward the parking lot, "are you going to tell me about the mysterious murderer?"

It had been hard enough telling it to the police today, realizing with every word that she was in some way betraying Zac, telling other people what she had refused to share with the person dearest to her heart. "Don't you have to go to work or something?" she asked.

"Not if you don't." Carl smiled at her. "But then, you're changing the subject on me."

"Carl, I . . . "

"Look, if you're truly in danger, then I'll be better prepared to help you if you tell me what's going on."

He had a point. She had to tell him something. "Just settle for this," she said. "There's a man, Steve, who blames me for breaking up his marriage and sending him to jail. This was almost ten years ago. I don't know why he's suddenly decided to seek revenge, but he has. I've heard his voice on the phone, and he left me that note at school. He's a violent man. He killed Bess, and he wants to kill me too." Her words brought home to Cecile just what kind of trouble she was in.

"Carl, you should know that you may be in danger if you try to help me," she continued reluctantly. If she scared Carl off, she would be truly alone. But she couldn't in good conscience let him help her without telling him what he was up against.

"I'm not suddenly going to turn faint-hearted on you," he assured her.

"You don't believe me, do you?"

"Of course I believe you! What's not to believe?" He looked sincere. "The only thing I question is your interpretation of the events," he went on, and Cecile's heart sank. "I have a hard time believing that what I saw was not suicide. But I can certainly understand your reluctance to accept that, particularly if this guy's been harassing you."

Cecile thought about retorting, then decided against it.

"Now," Carl said, "let's get some breakfast, and then I'll take you home."

It was almost noon when they arrived back at the apartment complex. Carl retrieved Cecile's suitcase from his apartment and loaded it into the trunk for her. Then, he held the door for her as she got into her car. He was trying hard to be nice.

"Why don't I follow you over to Zac's?" he asked. "Just to make sure you get there all right?"

She rolled her eyes. "I don't think Steve's going to attack me while I'm driving over there. Really, I'll be fine."

Carl looked dubious, but he shrugged. "Okay, if you're sure. You have my cell phone number, right?"

She patted the pocket where she had put the number. "I've got it right here."

"Remember, you can call me anytime, day or night. I'll keep that phone with me wherever I go, and I'll keep the line open."

"Thanks, Carl. I really do appreciate all of this."

"It's my pleasure," he assured her, laying his hand lightly

on her shoulder. After a gentle squeeze, he closed the door for her, then stood back.

Biting her lip, she put the car in reverse and backed out of the space. Carl was still watching her with that concerned expression on his face. She smiled at him, then drove off, refusing to look back.

With Carl out of sight, she could relax a little. When she was close by him, it seemed almost as if there were a rubber band around them. It was impossible to pull away, to break his spell.

She wondered how Zac was doing. She would have to call George and let him know where she was staying. And she would have to go to the hospital today to visit.

The drive to Zac's apartment took about ten minutes. She let herself in, and sighed at the sight of the mess. She couldn't live in such disorder; she was going to have to clean it up.

She placed the slip of paper with Carl's phone number next to the kitchen phone, then went into Zac's bedroom to change. The bag Carl had packed for her contained only skirts and dresses, mostly short ones, none of them suitable for housework. She imagined he had rummaged through her drawers and closets looking for items he would like to see her wearing. After stowing her clothes in the closet for later use, she changed into a pair of Zac's rattiest shorts and a torn, oversized t-shirt.

She started with the kitchen, gathering the empty frozen food containers into a trash bag, then emptying the dishwasher and sluicing down the counters and the stove. She was about to move on to the living room when she decided the floor needed mopping. She smiled to herself. She'd never before thought of housework as therapeutic, but the quest for perfection, coupled with the physical labor, pushed worries and fears to the back of her mind, granting her a temporary oblivion. The reprieve was so welcome that it was past dinner time when she finally had to admit that the place was spotless.

Sweating and stinking of any number of chemical cleaners, she toured the apartment, wiping off imaginary specks of dust, pulling individual dog hairs off the furniture. The place probably hadn't been this clean when Zac had first moved in!

Cecile didn't even mind the way her muscles ached and quivered, or the harsh, sandpaper texture of her hands. She went into the bathroom and turned on the water for a shower, then undressed, and stepped in as steam filled the room. Water as hot as she could bear washed the sweat and grime from her body, relaxing and soothing her tired muscles.

She basked in the heat and didn't leave the shower until her fingers and toes had reached an advanced state of prunehood and the hot water was running out. Sighing in satisfaction, she wrapped herself in a towel and went toward the kitchen for a drink of water.

As she passed through the combined living room/dining room, her eyes were drawn toward the dining room table. When she had dusted it, she had cleared everything off its surface. Now there was something sitting on the table.

Cecile clutched the towel tightly around herself, and slowly approached the table, trembling. She reached out and picked up the bottle that was standing there, the bottle that certainly had not been there when she had finished cleaning, the bottle of amber fluid that was clearly alcoholic, though Zac didn't drink. Her mouth gone dry, she turned the bottle to see the label.

Suddenly, Cecile lost control of both her hands, one letting the towel slip off, the other releasing the bottle so that it crashed to the floor, sending shards of glass and splashes of Dewars all over the pristine room and all over her legs.

Breathing in short gasps, Cecile hastily retrieved the towel and wrapped it around her, eyes frantically scanning the room. Was he still here? Had that coat closet door been open when she took her shower? She didn't think so. She edged toward the kitchen, her eyes fixed on the open closet door. Someone was in there, watching her, waiting. She sensed it.

In the kitchen, she grabbed the biggest, sharpest knife she could find, and held it in front of her as she reached for Carl's phone number. The Scotch-soaked towel dropped once more to the floor. Cecile read the number, then took the receiver off the hook and let it dangle while she dialed with her left hand, still holding the knife with her right.

Carl answered on the first ring.

"Carl, help me," she said, her voice quivering.

"I'm on my way," he said, voice edgy with alarm. She could hear him opening and closing the door to his apartment. "What's wrong?" he asked.

"I think he's here."

"Steve?"

"Yes."

"You *think* he's there?"

"In a closet. He . . . He . . . "

"I'll be right over, honey. Stay calm. If he's really there in the apartment, I doubt he'd have let you get to the phone." She heard the sound of his car starting. "Okay, how do I get there?"

As she gave Carl directions, her heartbeat began to calm. Of course he was right. If Steve were in the closet, he would have come out by now. He had left the closet door open just to scare her that much more. Maybe he had hoped she would go running into the street stark naked. He was toying with her, enjoying her fear. When he decided to stop playing, she would have no warning.

"I'm going to put the phone on the seat beside me," Carl

said, "but I'm not going to hang up. You just keep the line open and holler if you're in trouble. Okay?"

"Okay," she whispered. She heard him put down the phone. It would take him just a few more minutes. She looked down at herself. It wouldn't do to be naked when he arrived.

Leaving the phone off the hook, she picked up the towel and moved slowly toward the bedroom, the knife poised in front of her, her eyes glued to the closet door.

Once in Zac's room, she locked the door, knowing that the button lock would offer no protection. She lifted the phone to be sure she still had a connection, and, hearing the roar of a car engine, hastily pulled on some clothes.

"Cecile?" the phone squawked at her.

Buttoning her skirt, she picked up the phone in one hand and the knife in the other. "Yes?"

"You all right?"

"I'm fine. You're right; I'm sure he's long gone by now."

"I'm pulling into the parking lot right now," he said.

"I'll come out to meet you." With Carl right outside, she felt confident enough to hang up.

Carefully, she opened the bedroom door, knife in hand just in case. She crossed through the living room, pushing the coat closet door closed as she passed. She heard Carl's footsteps on the landing.

Carl knocked on the front door, and Cecile let him in. He glanced at the knife in her hands as he entered, and backed up a step, raising his eyebrows comically. "I hope that's not for me!" he said. He reached out his hand and she handed the knife to him. "Which closet did you think he was in?"

"I'm sure he's not there."

"I'll check anyway."

She nodded toward the coat closet. Carl gently brushed

her aside and yanked open the door. As expected, there was no one there. He moved aside all the coats, to be sure. He methodically searched the rest of the apartment, and only then did he ask Cecile what had convinced her Steve was in the closet. She explained as she began cleaning up the shattered glass.

"You're sure the bottle wasn't there before?"

"I'm positive," she said. "Besides, Zac doesn't drink, and that's the same brand that Steve always liked. He was here, Carl."

"We should call the police again."

She considered that thought, then rejected it. "Somehow I can't imagine them making much of a bottle of Scotch appearing on the table."

"Maybe not. But it's clear Steve can get into this apartment. If I have to drag you off kicking and screaming I will. You are *not* staying here alone."

Certainly that was out of the question. She could check into a hotel, but Steve had found her at Zac's, and could just as easily get to her at a hotel. Nowhere was safe.

"Stay at my place, Cecile," Carl urged. "Please. I'll sleep on the sofa."

She nodded.

7

There was a large wooden chest in one corner of the cabin. From it, Ariadne produced a heavy fur coat, along with a hat, boots, and gloves. "I have no scarf for you," she said. "You'll need to pull your shirt up over your nose. I don't want any of your parts falling off from frostbite."

Zac cringed at the thought of going back out into that cold. Though the frostbite had been healed, he remembered vividly how it had felt while setting in, remembered the horrible ache in his head and lungs. The furs that Ariadne was providing would help, but not for long, not in that preternatural cold.

"How far do we have to go?" he asked.

"Far enough," was her terse answer.

As he girded himself in fur, Ariadne poured him another vial of her magic brew. He bolted it down, grimacing once again at the awful taste. She poured the remains of the kettle into a flask, which she slipped into a pocket inside her cloak.

The howls of the wind seemed louder to Zac, and even draped in furs in this fire-heated room, chills passed through him. How much more suffering would he have to endure before this was over? How long before his will gave out? He was not a brave man; there was only so much he could take.

"Don't you have any furs for yourself?" he asked.

"My flesh is not subject to the same rigors as yours," she said, taking hold of the doorknob. "Now, are you ready?"

"No. But I never will be."

She snorted. "With those heroic words, we launch our noble quest." She flung open the door, and a gust of frigid air burst in, snuffing out the fire like a candle.

Ariadne stepped into the snow and beckoned impatiently, and Zac willed himself to follow. The cold quickly enveloped him, penetrating deeply, finding its way through to his flesh. He wondered whether his dense furs were helping at all. The thin shirt he had pulled over his face seemed to offer little protection.

Lowering his head against the wind, he followed Ariadne. Her form was ghostly and insubstantial in the swirling snow. Her feet seemed not to sink as deeply, and her steps came without effort. Her cloak, billowing in the wind, gave brief glimpses of her bare skin.

It wasn't long before the effects of the warming drink had faded and Zac had sunk into a misery so deep he was tempted to lie down in the snow and let it cover him, as he had once before. What was the point of continuing? His legs already ached from the strain of forcing his way through the drifts. He wouldn't make it much farther.

He slowed, and finally stopped. Ariadne noticed, and, walking lightly over the snow, approached.

"Don't tell me you're growing faint at heart yet again!" she said.

Zac shivered and hung his head. "I just need a rest."

"Well you can't have one. Standing still in this cold isn't going to help you. And don't expect me to carry you back to the cabin if you collapse again."

Zac wondered if she meant it. How important was it to

her that he reach the center of the labyrinth and face Carcajou? When she had exhorted him to travel farther into the depths of the labyrinth, her commitment to the mission had burned in her eyes; but now she seemed willing to let it fail any time he wavered. Or was it just that she knew she had already won? Zac would never find it in himself to call her bluff; why then *should* she coddle and cajole him?

"Perhaps I shouldn't have bothered with you," she sneered. "I should have waited for a *real* man. You lose your nerve every few minutes."

Zac felt no surge of manly indignation. Had her goading, for once, missed its mark? Or was he no longer capable of feeling anything but despair? He lowered his head once more and continued forward.

Somewhere along the way, he lost his sense of time. His mind drifted on its own, driven like the snow, searching out memories of a time before he had ever heard the names Ariadne and Carcajou. He thought of Cecile, lying on his bed, asleep in his arms for the first time. He thought of George, sniffing disdainfully and telling him what a loser he was, and of Bess, beautiful, sexy Bess, who, for whatever reason, aroused no interest in him. Then he thought again of Cecile, this time sitting on the edge of his bed, crying; crying because she had wanted to give herself to him and found that she could not. He wanted her still, no matter that Ariadne had stolen his innocence, no matter that the physical experience with Cecile could never be the same as it had been with Ariadne.

That thought startled him. He hadn't allowed himself to think it before. How badly had Ariadne poisoned him? Was he condemned to think of her any time he was with Cecile? In a way, it would serve him right. He had vowed to himself that he would remain faithful to Cecile, even in his dreams. It was his penance now to remember, to regret, to repay.

He became aware of a strange sensation. At first he couldn't place it. Something was happening to him, but what? Where was he? The world seemed to be moving.

"Snap out of it, already!" Ariadne's voice pierced the fog in his head, and he realized the world was *not* moving. It was his head snapping back and forth as she shook him, slapped him, brought him out of his stupor. His thoughts returned to the present, and the cold came rushing back into him. The snow still swirled and stung.

They were standing on the top of a massive mound of snow, knee-deep in soft powder. Before them lay an expanse of smooth, white-dusted ice, stretching as far as the eye could see. In the distance, marring the smooth purity of the icy surface, was a perfectly round, black hole. His stomach flipped in a familiar manner. That was the entrance to the next level.

Ignoring his nervous system's warnings, he began clambering down the hill toward the ice. *This* time, he was going on to the next level without Ariadne's prodding, without her mockery and threats. It couldn't be any worse than this place. He slipped and slid his way down the hill, falling only once before reaching the bottom. Ariadne easily followed behind.

Holding his arms out for balance, Zac slid his foot along the ice toward the distant hole. The wind gusted strongly, and his feet slid out from under him, landing him on his butt with a painful thump. Ariadne, gracefully striding past him, laughed out loud.

"You haven't the grace nor the balance to walk to the hole, Hamlet dear. I'm afraid you'll have to crawl."

He pretended to ignore her and struggled to his feet. She was probably right; the gusting wind would send him down to the ice many more times, especially in his exhausted state.

But he was damned if he was going to crawl!

He managed four more steps before another blast of wind knocked him down.

Ariadne shook her head. "Eventually, you'll have to start listening to me," she said. "I would have thought by now you'd have abandoned your macho pride. How many times do you suppose you'll be able to pick yourself back up?"

"As many times as I need to," he said, rising to his feet once more.

Ariadne grunted with disgust, then suddenly hooked her foot around his ankle and pulled, sending him back to the ice. "We'll try one more time to make you listen to reason," she said. "You'll need all the strength you can muster to reach the next level. If you're too stubborn to conserve your energy, I'll do it for you."

Filled with a sudden fury, Zac tried to kick her legs out from under her, but she dodged his flailing foot nimbly. His hands clenched into fists, and he imagined what it would feel like to have her flesh within those hands, to squeeze her until she cried out in pain and agreed to let him walk to his destiny, not crawl like an animal. He remembered what it had felt like when his knuckles had connected with the soft skin and hard bone of her cheek, and he wanted to feel it again, wanted to feel the shiver that traveled all the way up his arm as that bone gave way to the crushing power of his fist. He had never before understood what it was to hate, how it clouded your mind, changed your perceptions, changed *you*. Closing his eyes tightly, unclenching his fists, breathing deeply and calmly, he swallowed back the bile.

His heart slowed its pounding rhythm, and he opened his eyes once more to find Ariadne squatting inches away. The wind was whipping her hair around her face in all directions, obscuring her expression.

"You'll have to confront it eventually," she yelled over the howls of the wind. "If what you fear most is what's in the unplumbed depths of your heart, then that's what you'll have to face to win your way to the center. If and when you escape the labyrinth, you will not be the same man who entered."

"I know that," he said. Hadn't he already changed? Hadn't a part of him already been broken? Would the man who emerged from this hell be a man Cecile still could love?

Never mind that. He dared not look so far ahead. For now, there was only the present. Ariadne would not let him walk to the hole. Very well, he would crawl. What did one more humiliation matter, anyway? No one would see but her, and she knew already how low he could sink.

Crawling on all fours, he started forward, Ariadne walking serenely beside him. He risked a glance up at her and saw how violently her hair and cloak writhed. The wind did seem less fierce closer to the ice.

The hole was closer now, and Zac was breaking out in a hot sweat beneath his thick furs. Dread flowed over him in waves, stronger and more daunting with every inch he gained, and he could not fight it back. Eyes closed, his heart drumming a frantic rhythm, his stomach clenching and un-clenching, he labored on. His hands and knees moved in con-cert, inching forward, until his groping, gloved fingers met with something so cold it seemed to freeze through them in an instant, sending shafts of ice into his veins. He gasped and pulled back, opening his eyes.

"You're here," Ariadne said from behind him.

It was the hole that he had touched, that had sent a paralyzing chill through fingers already too numb, he had thought, to feel anything at all. He removed his glove; the hand that had touched the hole showed no evidence of damage, though the fingers now burned fiercely.

He looked once more at the hole. What had seemed nothing more than inky blackness was really dark water, still and forbidding even in the wind.

"What do I do?" he asked Ariadne.

"You go in."

He stared at her.

"You need to drink this down first," she continued, holding out the flask she had brought from the cabin. "This transition won't be as easy as your others have been. You have to work to get through this doorway.

"When you get in the water, you must swim that way," she said, pointing. "You won't last long, so swim hard and fast."

"What do you mean, I won't last long?"

"You remember our discussion in the cabin, don't you?"

"You mean the 'undiscovered country?' I'm going to die?"

"Yes. It's the only way to the next level. What you must resolve to do is not die too quickly. Swim with all your strength, as far as you can, as straight as you can. If you get far enough, you will be dragged into the next level. If you don't . . . "

"I *stay* dead."

"Yes."

"And if I decide not to try at all?"

"Then you'll die here instead, more slowly, for I won't save you. If you back out on me now, I'll have no more use for you, will I?"

He nodded. He hadn't actually considered not going. He knew by now how limited his choices were, and he was prepared to do what he had to do.

"Give me the flask," he told her.

The first thing Cecile noticed when she and Carl pulled into the parking lot was that the door to her apartment was open. Carl gave her a worried look, but Cecile had already seen the silver Volvo parked near the stairway. "Bess's parents are here," she said. "That's their car."

"Do you want to go talk to them?"

She shuddered. "No."

Mr. and Mrs. Newman had never been overly fond of her. They were the sort of people who looked down their noses at those who were shy, thinking them cold and unfriendly, and though they had never said anything unkind, at least not in Cecile's presence, she sensed their disapproval whenever they came to visit Bess.

What would the Newmans think of her now? Surely the police would have told the grieving parents about the note they had found. How they must hate Cecile, blaming her for their daughter's death! She wasn't even sure she could bear to go to the funeral. "Let's get inside before they come out," she urged.

Carl hustled her into his apartment, and closed the door. He put his hands on her shoulders, massaging the tight spot where her neck and back met. As his fingers dug into the knots there, relaxing and finally releasing them, Cecile closed her eyes and allowed some of the tension to flow out of her. She had to stay on her guard with Carl, but this felt good. This felt very good.

"Have you had anything to eat?" he asked.

Her stomach rumbled at the question, and she shook her head. She hadn't eaten since their meager breakfast.

"I'm not much of a chef, I'm afraid," he said. "But I think I have enough ingredients in my pantry to whip up some pasta and sauce. Unless you'd prefer to go out?"

"No. Pasta sounds fine."

"Good. Why don't you have a seat while I cook." He directed her to his sofa. "Just lean back and rest your eyes awhile. I won't be long."

Cecile did as he suggested, but the moment she closed her eyes, she thought of all the things she *should* be doing right now. She should have the courage to go and talk to the Newmans. She should call the police and let them know where she was staying, in case they had any news. She should visit Zac in the hospital—even if he wouldn't know she was there.

Unable to find peace with her thoughts, she paced the living room as Carl clattered around in the kitchen. Why hadn't she visited Zac this afternoon, when she'd had all the time in the world? She should have been by his side, supporting him, not cleaning his apartment in a futile attempt to forget. She glanced at her watch and realized it was now past visiting hours. She had squandered her chance.

Carl heard her pacing, and appeared in the kitchen doorway. "What's up?" he asked.

"I'm just trying to work up the courage to go talk to Bess's folks. I have to find out when the funeral is. And I have to say *something* to them."

He came toward her, flinging a kitchen towel over his shoulder. "Not now you don't. First you've got to stop blaming yourself for what happened. No one in their right minds would think it was your fault."

"Grieving parents are rarely in their right minds."

"True," he conceded, "but you don't have to face them now. I'll go talk to them, if they're still there, while the water's heating up."

A hard, painful lump formed in Cecile's throat. She should go herself. She knew that. She had been Bess's roommate and her friend, and Carl had barely known her.

"Give yourself a little time, Cecile. You need it, and you deserve it. I'll be back in a minute." He didn't wait for her consent this time, heading directly for the door, kitchen towel still over his shoulder.

She didn't try to stop him. She was already on the verge of collapse, as if any moment now she would start screaming and never stop. Could she hold herself together long enough to get through all of this? She sagged down onto the sofa, and waited.

When the door opened, Cecile started and almost screamed. Carl held up a placating hand. "It's just me," he said. "I caught them on their way out. The funeral's the day after tomorrow at 11 A.M. I wrote down the address for you."

"Thank you so much, Carl. I feel so helpless, but . . . "

"Hey, you're holding up as well as could be expected; now just hang in there. I'll be right back; I've got to put the pasta on."

He disappeared into the kitchen for a minute, then returned and sat beside Cecile on the couch. He stroked her hair, and Cecile rested her head against his shoulder, not caring what signal she was sending. He was the only one who was here when she was most desperately in need.

"Maybe the best thing would be for you to get away for a while," Carl murmured. "To the mountains, or the beach. I'd go with you. Separate rooms, of course."

How good it would feel to get away from here, to just run away from her troubles, if only for a little while! She shook her head.

"Uh oh, you're worrying about something," he said. "You get that little crease between your eyes when you're trying to find a good excuse to refuse me." He touched her forehead where she knew that crease existed.

She tried to extricate herself from his arm, but he was sitting too close, leaning into her ever so slightly, intruding on her space.

"Listen, Carl," she said. "The truth is, I'd like nothing better than to run away right this second. But you know I can't. I have to go to Bess's funeral, and I've got to be here for Zac, and I've got to wait and hear what the police find out about Steve's whereabouts. And I don't know how long I can stay away from school without getting fired. I can't just run away."

"You're right, I was being stupid. But maybe on the weekend? A day or two away from all this stress? Might be just what you need."

"I'll think about it."

"Let me call around and make us a reservation for somewhere."

"Oh Carl, *please* let me think about it."

"Perhaps you'd be better off if you did a little less thinking," he said softly. "Either you trust me or you don't trust me; make up your mind which it is."

Cecile could think of nothing to say. There was a distinct touch of frost in the air as Carl removed his arm from her shoulders and inched away from her on the couch.

"I can't trust you, Carl," she finally whispered. "Please forgive me. You know so little about me. I have a very hard time trusting any man. It's not just you, and I know you don't deserve it."

What a hypocrite she was being! It *was* him, and she knew it.

"All right," Carl said. "I can accept that. I've done my best to accept what you're willing to give. But please accept that I'm not a good enough actor to hide my feelings all the time."

Cecile looked up and met his eyes, and they pulled her in. He was leaning toward her again, his drawn-back hair accentuating his sharp good looks. His lips were parted slightly, as if in anticipation of a kiss. Cecile felt her pulse quicken in her throat, imagined what his lips would feel like against hers. His tongue would taste of cinnamon and coffee and his skin would smell faintly of aftershave.

Her breathing came shallow as he leaned closer, so close his two eyes blurred into one, so close she felt the warmth of his breath on her cheek. She tried to pull away, to stand up, to turn her head, but she was frozen. His breath brushed her lips and her eyes slid closed.

She felt the heat of him for a tantalizing moment, her body rigid with conflict, unable to decide whether she wanted him to back away, or to press his body against hers, filling her with his strength and confidence. Then the heat receded as she felt him slide away from her on the couch and stand up. She swallowed hard, whether with regret or relief she wasn't sure.

She opened her eyes. Carl was standing with his back to her, rubbing the back of his head.

"I'm sorry, Cecile," he said. "Here I am telling you to trust me, and I can't keep from making a pass at you two seconds later." His words were tight and clipped, as if it hurt to utter them.

What could she say to him? *Don't feel bad, I'm having trouble controlling myself too?* She barely knew him! What was it that made her want to do with him what she couldn't do with Zac, what she had sworn to herself as a frightened adolescent she would never do with any man, lest she recall the horrifying, humiliating moment when Steve had pinned her face down on the bed, when she had known it was hopeless, that she had lost? Tears brimmed in her eyes, and she could find no words to break the silence.

Carl stood there, his back still turned. Finally, he turned back to her.

"Perhaps you were right all along," he said. "Perhaps you

should stay somewhere else. "

Cecile's chest tightened and she shot to her feet. "No!" She took two hasty steps in Carl's direction and grabbed his arms, daring once more to look into his eyes. "Please don't make me go! Steve will find me. I'm sorry I'm sending you mixed signals; I swear I'm not doing it on purpose. I'm just so confused and so alone. Please. You're the only friend I have left."

Carl's expression softened and he pulled Cecile into his arms. "All right," he said into her hair. "If you can take it, I can. I would never kick you out. I only meant that I thought you *wanted* to leave. You can stay as long as you like, and I promise no one will hurt you."

She pressed into his arms, so tight she felt the hard bulge in his jeans.

Abruptly, Carl let go. "I'd better check on dinner," he mumbled.

Cecile awoke, the book on her lap sliding to the floor with a loud thump. Groggy and disoriented, she looked at the clock beside Carl's bed. 2:45. She stretched, her back and neck stiff from the cramped position in which she had fallen asleep.

She had pleaded exhaustion at about 11:30, needing to get away from Carl awhile, to give her mind and body just a touch of relief. He had not challenged her, instead making up his own bed on the sofa and inviting her to choose a book to read, in case she should have trouble sleeping. His collection of books had unnerved her: a strange combination of thrillers, horror novels, and erotica, along with works by Machiavelli and de Sade.

She had taken one of the more innocuous-looking thrillers. She had no intention of actually reading the book, but once

inside Carl's bedroom, she had found herself completely disinclined to undress and get into bed. She had locked the door
and sat in an armchair in the corner to read.

She had no idea what time she'd fallen asleep, nor what
had awakened her, though she had vague memories of nightmares. Now she began undressing, pleased that Carl had
packed a nightgown for her. How like him it would have
been to "accidentally" overlook that particular item.

Did Steve know she was staying in Carl's apartment? He
seemed to know any number of things he shouldn't. What
smug satisfaction he must be feeling; pure, innocent Cecile,
spending the night in the apartment of a man she barely
knew. Steve had always claimed her innocence was an act,
that inside her was a wanton waiting to escape. He'd said that
to her after she had caught him with his girlfriend.

Her thoughts went back to that night. She was staying
with a neighbor, only two doors down from her own house.
Her mother was away, visiting a friend from college. Steve
was supposed to be away too, on business; at least that was
the excuse he gave for not accompanying her mother.

At bedtime, Cecile realized that she had forgotten her
toothbrush, and ran home to get it, planning to let herself in
the back door. That was when she noticed Steve's car, impossible to see from the road because of the hedges. Had Steve
been anyone else, she might have imagined any number of
innocent explanations for his being there. In reality, all her
thoughts were damning. She walked to the door, keys in
hand, and stood there.

Instinct told her that the next few moments could change
the course of her life. She could turn away, go back to the
neighbor's house, forget about brushing her teeth just this
once. Or, she could open the door and find out once and for
all whether her suspicions were justified.

Muffling the jingle of her keys, Cecile unlocked the door. She tiptoed into the hall, quietly closing the door behind her. Then she heard the sounds, sounds that were immediately recognizable, and yet wholly alien to her. Heavy breathing. Rhythmic creaking. Soft moans and heavy grunts. She knew what she was hearing, knew she had the proof she needed. But something compelled her, kept her creeping through the hall toward the living room from which the sounds emanated. She had to see. Had to, though her heart seized up with fear—of what, she did not then know. A few more steps, and she would be at the corner. The moans and grunts grew louder, the breathing more labored. She reached the corner and peeked into the room.

The woman was lying chest-down on the couch. Her face was turned away from Cecile; her strawberry blonde hair, soaked with sweat, was draped over the edge of the sofa, brushing the floor; and her arms were stretched over her head, bracing her against the side of the sofa. She was wearing clothes, but her skirt was flung up over her back, and her panties were down around one ankle. Steve was naked astride her, teeth clenched in a grimace of pleasure, heavy-lidded eyes almost closed. His knuckles were white with strain, so tightly was he gripping the woman's shoulders; but she uttered no protest.

Riveted in guilty fascination, Cecile stood in the doorway. She had seen graphic scenes in a few movies; but nothing had prepared her for this. The brutish force of it, the animal sounds, the pungent odor that permeated the air; the woman's face, forgotten and unimportant, buried in the cushions of the sofa.

Steve must have sensed her presence, must have known that someone was watching his utter conquest of the nameless woman. He looked up suddenly, and met Cecile's eyes. While she remained transfixed, he redoubled his efforts, and the woman howled in what could have been pain or pleasure or both.

The cry broke the spell, and Cecile was able to turn away, fleeing back to the safety of her neighbor's house.

Steve had shown up the next morning, ostensibly to take Cecile with him, grocery shopping. It was all she could do to get into the car with him and not make a scene in front of her neighbors, and she avoided looking at him.

The memory of that car ride haunted her still. Steve's easy confidence and utter lack of remorse or guilt. The way he abandoned his facade of civility and threw around words like "fuck." The way she sat silently, red-faced, as Steve asked her how long she had watched, what she had felt, and whether she had enjoyed it. It was only after he had gotten his fill of taunting and humiliating her that he had issued the dire threats that she now wished she'd heeded.

Cecile tried to dispel the vivid memory. Why was she letting herself think about it? For so long she had successfully pushed these memories to a back corner of her mind. Now, they had slipped past her defenses.

She slid into Carl's bed and turned off the light. She fluffed the pillow, then snuggled comfortably into it, breathing in its spicy, musky scent, the scent she had come to associate with Carl. How gallant he had been today, driving to her rescue the moment she had called. Even if he did have ulterior motives, it was comforting to know that he was in the next room, ready to come running should she need him.

Outside the bedroom window, something made a faint clicking noise. Cecile's hand clenched the covers. Her whole body rigid with tension, she lay still, straining her ears. Was someone out there?

You can't keep starting at every noise! she told herself. But the tension remained, and as she listened intently, she heard another noise, like fingernails scraping over glass. She sat bolt upright and flicked on the light switch, her hands shaking. Carl was just outside, she reminded herself. She was not alone. But she had locked the bedroom door!

She slipped out of the bed, her eyes fixed on the window, expecting the glass to shatter at any moment. Her breath came in quick gasps, as she reached the door and opened it and slipped into the living room.

Carl lay asleep on the sofa, one arm tossed up over his eyes, the other hanging over the edge, fingertips brushing the floor. His lips were parted slightly, and his naked chest rose and fell slowly. Cecile stepped toward him, meaning to wake him. Then she stopped.

Carl had already come rushing to her rescue once today. Even if the noises had come from Steve, surely he was long gone by now.

She wiped her sweaty palms on her nightgown. Her pulse slowing, she crept back into the bedroom, leaving the door unlocked this time, and slightly ajar. Then, the light still on, she climbed back into Carl's bed and breathed again of his scent on the pillows.

Zac took as deep a breath as the cold would allow, then poured the draught down the back of his throat. He gagged, and thought his stomach would revolt. Then, the nausea faded, replaced by spreading warmth.

"You must hurry," Ariadne urged. "The drug's protection won't last long."

He moved toward the hole in the ice, but she seized a handful of his collar and jerked him to a halt.

"Take off your clothes," she commanded.

He just blinked at her as a gust of icy wind tore through

him. The thought of leaving his skin bare to the lash of the wind froze his heart.

"How do you expect to swim with thirty pounds of water-soaked clothes dragging at you with every stroke?"

Still he hesitated.

"The coat and clothing will offer no protection from the water anyway!"

Zac gritted his teeth and hurriedly began to strip. The warmth of the drug was already receding.

"Swim as hard as you can, to the north, Hamlet," Ariadne said. She pointed to indicate the direction. "Use all of your energy. When you feel your breath running out, don't let yourself panic. You must keep swimming until the very last moment when you cannot help but breathe the water. If you don't get far enough, you'll never breathe air again. Do you understand?"

"I understand!" he yelled, his whole body shaking with the cold. He discarded the last of his clothing. Then, his stomach cramped with fear, he pinched his nose and stepped off the edge of the ice.

Nothing could have prepared him for the shock that sliced through him. He almost sucked a lungful of water in the first instant, so strong was his body's need to gasp. The water seeped into his eyes, into his ears. Every second, fingers of ice seemed to penetrate more deeply: now digging into the thin layer of fat under his skin; now piercing the fat, and plucking at the muscle beneath, burrowing through to his bones, to his heart, to his brain. Cold fire scalded his lungs. His head banged against the ice above him, and his hands flailed, desperately seeking the hole through which he had come. But the hole was sealed.

Hopelessly disoriented, he tried to move his arms and legs, tried to kick and stroke, but there was no feeling. His heart thudded violently in his chest, and the burning in his lungs escalated as his body used the last dregs of oxygen from his bloodstream. He had to get out of here. Had to!

He ran his hands along the ice above him, banging on it, looking for a weakness. The banging restored some feeling to his arms—a feeling as if one more blow would shatter them into shards. Then, once again, he felt nothing, and he could only guess whether he was hitting the ice, or whether his body was sinking deeper and deeper into the abyss. Spots of brilliant color flared in his eyes, but he knew they were illusion, knew there was nothing, knew he was alone here in the darkness.

Of course, he had always been alone. Even with the one he loved, he hadn't been able to share the secrets of his soul, and when he had tried, she had turned from him, frightened and appalled. She had loved the Zac she thought she knew, but the true man had been foreign to her, a creature so bizarre it had to be held at bay. Was that why she hadn't been able to enjoy physical intimacy with him? Was she recoiling from the truth of him, from the threat his alien soul posed to her peace of mind?

How fitting now, in the moment of his death, that he should be so utterly alone; so alone that the aloneness became a part of his being, became his reason for being. And then became his reason for *not* being. What was the point of fighting, if all he could win was the chance to be alone again? He would never change; he would never be one of "them," one of the *normal* people, who lived *normal* lives, and had *normal* fantasies, fantasies about the girl next door; about what they would say to their boss if only they had the nerve. How did you relate to people like that, when your own fantasies ruled your life—and were capable of causing your death? No, the connections that tied him to the real world were tenuous at best, tied to other people's ideas of who he was. The world would suffer no great loss if he ceased to exist.

Zac welcomed the water into his lungs.

8

Cecile woke to the sound of a coffee cup being placed on the bedside table, and faint memories of erotic dreams. She glanced at the clock and saw that it was 7:15.

"Sorry to wake you this early," Carl said, standing beside the bed in silk pajama bottoms, a different pair this time. "I figured you'd need to call your school to tell them you won't be in."

She sat up and reached for the coffee. Her head ached from lack of sleep and she wasn't yet ready to face the day.

"Did you sleep all right?" he asked.

She shrugged. "I suppose so. How about you? Was the couch miserable?"

"Nah. It's a great couch for sleeping. I slept like a baby."

She sipped the coffee. It was far better than anything Bess ever made, and Carl had added just the right amount of milk and sugar. "I should go in to work today," she said, half-heartedly.

"No. You need some time off. You should ask for a leave of absence."

Cecile recoiled at the thought. The school year had just begun, and she'd already missed time due to "illness." Requesting a leave would try Mrs. Stanhope's patience.

On the other hand, she would do no one any good at school like this. How could she possibly concentrate? She couldn't, plain and simple. Mrs. Stanhope had a well-earned reputation for intolerance when it came to teachers with troubled personal lives, but Cecile would have to face her anyway. "It's not going to be easy," she muttered.

"Nothing's going to be easy right now," Carl said. "All you can do is find the path that's least difficult." He moved the bedside phone closer to Cecile, then took the receiver off the hook and handed it to her. "Don't sit here and stew about it. Just make the call and get it over with."

Cecile desperately wanted to finish her coffee first, but she dialed. Carl patted her knee through the covers, then tactfully left her alone, shutting the bedroom door behind him.

The school phone rang three times before Clare answered. Cecile said, "May I speak to Mrs. Stanhope, please?"

"Cecile, is that you?"

"Yes."

"How are you feeling?"

"Uh . . . better. Can you put me through to Mrs. Stanhope?"

"Sure. But I should warn you, Chuckles is in one of her moods today."

Cecile's stomach lurched. "Do you think I should call back some other time?"

"Up to you. How important is it?"

Not that important, she thought. It's only my job on the line—a trivial concern, with my roommate dead, my boyfriend in a coma, and a killer stalking me.

But someday this would all end and life would return to normal and she would need her job. "I guess you'd better put me through to her now. There's no telling when she won't be in 'one of her moods' again."

Clare giggled, then put Cecile on hold. The phone tapped into the local classical music station, which was broadcasting the Rite of Spring. The chaotic pulses of sound were unsettling, like monsters in a horror movie, popping out of dark, quiet corners when least expected. Suddenly the pulses came to a halt, and Mrs. Stanhope was on the other end of the line. "Yes?" she said, making no effort to hide her irritation.

Cecile cleared her throat, buying a little time to compose herself. With all that had happened, it was ridiculous to be frightened of Mrs. Stanhope! "This is Cecile," she said.

"Yes, I know." The impatience in her voice escalated.

"Umm . . . I'm afraid I need to request a leave of absence."

"Oh?" Cecile could almost hear Mrs. Stanhope's eyebrows raising. "For how long?"

"I'm not sure. I'd guess a couple weeks." There was a long silence on the other end of the phone, and Cecile knew the question she was dreading was about to be asked.

"And for what reason do you need this leave?"

Here was the perfect time to lie. If Cecile claimed there was a death in her family, Mrs. Stanhope might concede the need to attend to family business. The death of a roommate, however, would not, in the headmistress's mind, carry the same weight of responsibility. And it was only responsibility that would justify the request for a leave. Mrs. Stanhope made no concession to the frailties associated with emotions; one's emotions should always be kept to oneself, and one's duties performed regardless.

With an instinct that she was only now learning to trust, Cecile realized that she dare not lie. To Mrs. Stanhope, the lie was the pinnacle of evil, never to be condoned, and certainly not forgiven. Never mind that her own daughter lied almost constantly.

No, Cecile would not lie, but she at that moment determined that she would not tell the truth either. "I need it for personal reasons," she stated, hoping her voice sounded firm.

"Personal reasons? What exactly does that mean?"

"It means it's too personal for me to discuss. Mrs. Stanhope, I've hardly missed a day from the moment I started teaching. I've always been on time, I've never shirked any of my duties. And my students like me. I think I've earned a little trust."

"Cecile, this is not a question of trust." She made it sound like a distasteful word. "This is a question of protocol. When a teacher requests a leave of absence, it creates a disruption in the operation of this school. We all know that substitute teachers—even the best ones—can never fill the shoes of the regular teacher. Not only that, but each of our teachers is essential for the smooth administration of this school. When you cause this kind of a disruption, you have to have a very good reason—"

"I do," Cecile interrupted, but Mrs. Stanhope continued, as if she had heard nothing.

"The protocol for a leave of absence requires you to explain your request, so we can avoid being disrupted for frivolous reasons."

Cecile took a deep breath. "My reasons are not frivolous, I assure you. I understand what the protocol is, and I understand why. However, I'm asking that you just put 'personal reasons' in my file and leave it at that."

Was it possible to *hear* someone frown over the phone? "I'm afraid I'll need something more specific."

Cecile's resolve remained firm. "Well, I'm afraid I can't give you anything more specific." She could almost see Mrs. Stanhope's shocked outrage at her blatant insubordination. "All I can say is that it's highly personal, and it's not frivolous.

I could have lied to you and made up a good reason that would look better on my file, but I didn't. I hope that you'll consider that a sign of good faith. I enjoy teaching at Sarah Walden, and I hope that I can return when I'm able." There, she had said it; she had made it clear that she would not budge, that she would not be bullied, that she was willing to accept the consequences of her recalcitrance.

There was a silence on the line. Mrs. Stanhope was not used to people standing up to her. How would she react to this? Cecile could imagine anything from outright indignation to grudging admiration.

"Well," Mrs. Stanhope said, "we appear to have reached an impasse for the time being. Why don't you stop by my office after school so we can talk about it in person? I have a meeting that will last until about 5:30. We can meet then."

"I'm not sure I—"

"If I do grant your request, there'll be paperwork to fill out."

Cecile didn't know what to say. The paperwork could surely be dealt with in Clare's office, anytime; the only reason Mrs. Stanhope could have for forcing a face-to-face meeting today was that she was sure her aura of intimidation would prevail in person. If only Cecile didn't fear that she was right! "All right," she said, resigned. "I'll be there."

"Good. I hope you know that we would hate to lose you."

Cecile closed her eyes. "Yes, Mrs. Stanhope." Knowing her voice would start to quaver if she said one more word, she quickly hung up.

After a big swallow of coffee, Cecile climbed out of Carl's bed. The next hurdle of the day would be visiting Zac in the hospital. She had heard nothing from George. For all she knew, Zac could be out of the hospital by now; though she figured even George would have called her if anything so significant had happened. She picked out a skirt and blouse, then slid out of her nightgown.

As her nightgown hit the floor, the door opened and Carl took a step into the room. Cecile gasped and covered her breasts with her arms.

"Oops!" Carl said, ducking back out of the room and pulling the door shut. "Sorry, Cecile," he said through the closed door. "I thought you were still on the phone."

Cheeks blazing, and unsure of Carl's sincerity, Cecile hastily pulled her clothes on. "That's okay," she managed to say, but she was sure he could tell how unsettled she was.

When she thought there was a chance that she could meet Carl's eyes without blushing, Cecile ventured into the kitchen, where he was just buttering the last slice of toast. He handed her a plate with a healthy serving of scrambled eggs and toast, and she mutely accepted it, turning to go to the dining room.

"You're beautiful," Carl said softly to her back. "I just thought you should know that."

Her steps faltered. Searching for a reply, but finding none, she continued to the dining room, where she put her plate down and began to eat in silence. Carl sat across from her.

"I have to go visit Zac," she said when she had finished eating.

"All right. I'll drive you."

"I'm sure I can make it to the hospital and back without Steve jumping me. It's a very public place."

"Yes, but you'd have to park your car in the deck, and that won't be safe."

"Well, I'll call a cab, then. You do have a life of your own. I'm sure you have a few things to do, and I need to do *something* by myself without feeling threatened."

She had made up her mind, and Carl relented. "Okay, I guess I could use some groceries. But you're to come straight back here when you're finished at the hospital. Understood?"

"Understood."

Carl reached across the table and took her hand in his. "This will end soon enough," he said. "The police are looking for Steve this very moment, and when they can't find him it will make your story look more plausible. Then they'll start looking for him around here, and eventually they'll catch him. You just have to hold on till then."

"I'll try." She went into the living room to phone a cab.

Cecile approached the door to Zac's room, nervous. It had taken a while to locate him; he had been moved out of intensive care into a semi-private room.

She was sure George was around somewhere, but she hadn't seen him yet, and she didn't want to. Might he be in Zac's room even now? And if so, could she control her temper enough to be polite? She doubted it.

The door to Zac's room was ajar, and Cecile pushed it open. The bed nearest the door was unoccupied, though the sheets were rumpled. The curtain was drawn around the far bed. The nurse at the nurse's station had informed Cecile that there had been no change in Zac's condition, that he was stable. Thank goodness for that, at least.

Cecile peeked around the curtain and was startled to see another visitor. A lovely older woman sat at Zac's bedside, reading a magazine. Blonde hair of a shade that would have looked completely natural on a younger woman was immaculately fluffed and curled under at shoulder level. Smooth, matte-finish makeup hid any tell-tale wrinkles, though from the tight look of the skin, Cecile guessed that she had had a face-lift or two in the past. The shade of polish on her professionally manicured fingernails exactly matched her pressed pink jacket. She looked like any number of the mothers Cecile had met at Walden, perfect and plastic in that distinctively wealthy way.

The woman seemed to sense Cecile's scrutiny, looking up from her magazine and smiling, showing movie-star white teeth. "Hello," she said. "Are you here to visit Zac?"

"Um, yes, I'm Cecile."

The woman rose from her seat, dropping the magazine on a bedside table and reaching her hand out toward Cecile. "I'm so pleased to meet you, Cecile," she said. "I'm Mrs. Martins, Zac's mother."

Cecile shook Mrs. Martins' hand, at a loss for words. She hadn't been sure she could control herself around George, but at least she had been prepared for him. What a time to suddenly have to meet Zac's parents! At least she was respectably dressed. Thank goodness Carl hadn't packed her jeans and T-shirts.

"You must be Zac's lady-friend," Mrs. Martins continued. "I'm afraid he was keeping a bit of a secret from us, wasn't he?"

"I guess so." Why *hadn't* Zac told his parents about her?

Mrs. Martins reclaimed her seat at Zac's bedside and motioned for Cecile to take the other chair. "They tell me you're the one who found him like this."

Cecile nodded. "Yes. I should have made him go to the doctor before, but he was so insistent." Her eyes blurred with tears.

Mrs. Martins shook her head. "Don't blame yourself, dear. I know how stubborn he can be. Once he's made up his mind, nothing on earth can make him change it." She looked at Zac fondly, patting his hand, which lay outside the blanket.

Despite the tubes, he didn't look sick. He didn't have the sickly pallor Cecile had expected, nor did he look flushed or feverish. If she hadn't known better, she would have sworn that a light tap on the shoulder would awaken him.

"Will I get to meet Mr. Martins?" Cecile asked, hoping she sounded like she was looking forward to the possibility, rather than dreading it.

Mrs. Martins frowned ever so slightly. "Not right away, I'm afraid. Ed is in the middle of a very important case. He just couldn't take the time to fly out here." She smiled, but Cecile distinctly heard chagrin in her voice.

Mrs. Martins must have seen the disapproval on Cecile's face, for she hastened to clarify. "You've got to understand, Zac and he haven't always gotten along so well these past few years. Ed has a lot of mixed feelings to deal with." She reached over and stroked Zac's hair. "He's really very dear to us all," she said. "But he makes it very difficult. He can be brutal, you know."

"Brutal?" She looked down at the man she loved, the gentlest man she had ever known. It was hard to imagine a word that described him less.

Mrs. Martins reached into her purse and pulled out a tissue to dab at her eyes. She forced a smile. "What I meant was, Zac doesn't think much of the way we live, and he isn't shy about telling us so. We just want the best for him."

Cecile shifted uncomfortably in her chair. She should say something. But what? She knew almost nothing about the workings of Zac's family. He had been as reticent about them as she had been about her past. And she'd never been much good at comforting people in distress.

Mrs. Martins sniffled daintily, then tucked her tissue back into her purse. Not a drop of her mascara had been allowed to run. "I'm sorry, dear. I shouldn't be troubling you with our family problems."

"That's all right." Cecile wanted desperately to sit by Zac's side, where his mother was sitting, to take his hand and feel the warmth of it. But she could hardly ask his mother to move, and Mrs. Martins didn't seem inclined to offer.

"So, how long have you and Zac been seeing each other?" Mrs. Martins asked in an unnaturally cheery voice.

"About six months now, I'd say."

"Really? That long?" She shook her head. "I wish he had told us. I would have liked to have met you under different circumstances. Perhaps when he's better you can come and visit us for a weekend."

"Sure," Cecile agreed. If only Zac *would* get better, she would happily subject herself to what she was sure would be a strained and unpleasant visit.

"Tell me how you two met," Mrs. Martins continued.

"Um, I had . . . have a dog, a poodle." Cecile's throat tightened at the thought of poor Panta. "I used to take him to Pet Parlor to get groomed. Zac always did a particularly nice job with him."

"Oh," Zac's mother said, and Cecile could sense the older woman trying to maintain her open, friendly demeanor. Zac had said that his parents weren't overly enamored of his career choice. Perhaps she shouldn't have brought it up at all.

"Well," Mrs. Martins tried again, "not your stereotypical first meeting, now, was it?" The smile was back, but it looked tight and forced.

Cecile squirmed in her chair. At that moment, the door swung open, and George entered the room, looking harried. Dark circles shadowed his eyes, and he had clearly taken a few shortcuts in his morning grooming regimen. His hair wasn't quite as perfect as the last time Cecile had seen him, nor were his clothes as obviously calculated to impress. He stopped short when he saw her.

"Cecile!" he exclaimed. "I was just going to call you." He shifted his eyes away from her. "I'm sorry I didn't call you earlier. I've just been so busy, and so terribly worried. I've been at the hospital pretty much day and night."

"They have phones at the hospital," she retorted, anger forcing the words out of her. Being at the hospital all day hadn't stopped him from calling his parents!

"Er, yes, that's true. I, uh—"

Mrs. Martins cleared her throat softly, and they both turned to look at her. "Perhaps you should have this discussion elsewhere," she suggested, nodding toward Zac.

"Mother, he can't hear us," George said.

"Are you one hundred percent sure of that?"

George seemed on the verge of snapping at her, but thought better of it. "All right. Cecile, would you step outside with me?"

She nodded, and followed him out.

With the door closed behind them, George lowered his voice and said, "I'm sorry I didn't call you, but you must understand, this has been a very trying time for me."

"For you? Do you think this has been easy for me? I have a right to know what's happening to him, and you promised you would call if there was any change."

"There has been no change in his condition."

"Then why is he out of intensive care?"

"Because that sweatshop of his offers no benefits."

Cecile blinked, not following the turn in the conversation. "What do you mean?"

"I mean," George told her, "Zac has no insurance. I'm footing his bills while he's in here. Do you have any idea how expensive a hospital stay is?"

"Yes, but—"

"I can't afford for him to stay in intensive care when they've done everything they can for him there. We're still waiting for some test results, but it's pretty clear that whatever's wrong with him is a psychiatric problem. His condition is very stable. All we have to do is make sure he gets enough nourishment."

"So what you're saying is you're giving up on him."

"No, I'm not. But psychiatric care for the indigent is minimal, at best. I won't trust him to a state-run hospital."

"So what happens to him?"

"I have a spare bedroom in my house, and I've hired a nurse to take care of him while I'm at work. It's not cheap, but it beats the hospital."

"You're taking him home?"

"Yes. This evening, if all goes well. I don't know that I can do all that much for him, but I won't do him any harm, which is more than I can say for anyone else."

"Are you going to give him any treatment, or are you just going to bury him in the back of your house like the family embarrassment?"

George's face turned hard and cold. "I don't have time for this. I still have a lot of work to do before the room is ready. Give me a call in a day or two, and I'll arrange for you to come visit him if you want." He turned from her without another word and went back into Zac's room.

Cecile stood staring at the door. She knew she should go back in and try to smooth things over with George, but she also knew her temper might get the better of her once more. Sighing with regret, she went looking for a public phone to summon a cab.

9

The blackness was upon him, and a detached calm replaced the panic. Zac's consciousness drifted off at the whim of a sudden current and he felt only a floating sensation, strangely tangible and yet so obviously illusory. No more pain. No cold. No instinct to breathe.

Then, it no longer felt like floating. It was more like falling, from an unimaginable height, faster, faster . . . until suddenly the air slammed back into his chest with the force of a full-fisted blow. With desperate instinct, he tried to suck another breath, but a gout of water burst from his mouth, gagging and choking him. He was dragged from the water by the collar, then deftly flipped over and held by the ankles as he sputtered and retched, and, finally, breathed.

Breaths like sobs burned down his throat and into his aching, throbbing chest. Shivers ripped through him from head to toe, and through it all, the sound of laughter filtered into his head.

He was being held over the side of a boat—seemingly with no effort—by an enormously tall, gaunt old man. The man was naked, his body a patchwork of scars, wrinkles, and age spots, his beard nearly covering his genitals, his few remaining teeth showing yellow and rotten through his laughing lips.

The boat was a sturdy gondola, fashioned of dark wood. Several passengers sat along its edges, laughing at Zac's struggles. One man, short and burly, with a bristly black beard, held a long pole that reached into the water—presumably to the bottom, as the man appeared to be resting his entire weight on it.

The old man cocked his head quizzically. "You know," he said, "I do return to shore on a regular basis. You didn't have to swim after me."

The passengers laughed. "Maybe he doesn't have a coin," one of them suggested.

"This one needs no coin; his toll has been paid by another." The old man smiled, showing more of his rotten teeth. "So, my boy, do you seek passage on my boat, or would you rather swim?"

Zac turned his head toward the shore, on which paced hundreds upon hundreds of pale, bent people. Choruses of wails and moans drifted over the water, and those closest to the edge reached their arms toward the boat. Several ventured a few steps into the water, but none dared swim.

Zac knew now where he was. The old man was Charon, the ferryman who delivered the souls of the dead into Hades. The hundreds who desperately paced the shore were those who'd had no coin placed beneath their tongues before burial, coins with which they could pay the ferryman, and without which they were doomed to wander forever without rest.

It seemed Zac had indeed died, and was now making the passage to the afterlife. The only question was whether his death had been real, or an illusion of the Other Place.

"Well?" Charon said. "Answer quickly, or it's back in the water with you." He dipped Zac's head in the river to illustrate his point.

"All right!" Zac croaked. "Bring me aboard."

Charon hauled him onto the boat and reclaimed his pole. Muscles rippled through his skeletal frame as he dipped the heavy pole into the water in front of him and leaned his weight against it. The boat slid forward silently, the sounds of rippling water swallowed by the howling of the lost souls on the far shore.

The water over which the boat glided was black as pitch; the sky above—if sky it was—was equally black. Zac could discern no source of light anywhere, yet he could see—though only dimly. Shivering in the Stygian night, he sat up, wrapping his arms across his naked chest for warmth. The other passengers stared into the distance, eyes displaying mixes of fear and awe and anticipation. Zac followed their gazes to the far shore of the river, where a number of robed figures clustered, awaiting the boat's arrival.

As the cries of the doomed behind them faded into an unnerving memory, the ferryman poled in perfect rhythm, effortless strokes that pushed the boat along at a brisk pace until it nudged against a rickety pier that jutted into the river. The robed figures converged on the boat, faces hidden by black hoods. Each of them reached out to a passenger, drawing him forward into the darkness, into his ultimate fate.

Finally, the last of the figures reached for Zac, who followed along willingly, down a narrow, winding path, with blackness on either side. His will to fight his destiny had drained out of him with the water of the Styx. Either he was dead now, or he would soon meet his fate at the hands of Carcajou.

"You seem to have grown calm," his guide told him.

Recognizing the voice, Zac looked up. The hood that had concealed her face was now draped over Ariadne's shoulders.

It occurred to Zac that he should feel at least mildly surprised to see her, but somehow his mind felt too sluggish for even so minimal an emotion. "Yes," he said. "Dying can have that effect on you." His voice came out flat and toneless. "Are you taking me toward Carcajou? I don't have the queasy feeling in my stomach that I usually have when I'm moving toward him."

"You are very close. He knows now that your fear will not keep you away, so he prepares his final road block."

"Which is?"

"You'll see soon enough," she said. "Allow me to give you the tour first. After all, you may never encounter this place again. You can hope not to, anyway."

Zac managed a shrug, and mutely followed her. He came to an abrupt halt as they rounded a sharp bend. The path was no longer surrounded entirely by blackness.

Ariadne stood before a large window that spanned upwards into the darkness. She beckoned him to join her and look in. He did so with trepidation, suddenly aware of some emotions that had not been expunged.

The window offered a view of a lighted scene, much like a diorama at a natural history museum. A corpulent man stood bent over at the bottom of a hill, a huge boulder half-again his height poised before him. The man's hands rested on his knees, and his head was bent to his chest, long, unruly hair hiding his face from view. Zac would have thought it a true diorama, had he not seen the man's ribs heaving, seen him slowly raise his head, seen his awful face.

Never had he seen such an expression of pure, unadulterated agony. The man's lips were drawn back from his teeth in a hideous grimace, and blood dripped from his mouth where he had bitten his tongue. The left side of his face and his shoulder were a mass of purple-green bruises, crusted over with flaking callouses. As Zac watched, the man leaned his devastated shoulder and cheek against the boulder and it began to move. His muscles and bones made popping, ripping noises as the boulder creaked forward an inch or two.

That the man could even begin to move something so massive was beyond comprehension. Slowly, slowly, his hands worn raw and bloody, he rolled the boulder a little farther up the hill.

"Are you familiar with the story of Sisyphus?" Ariadne asked. Zac was too absorbed in the poor man's struggles to respond. "Sisyphus was a king of Corinth. He was a clever man, and he devised a plan whereby he could avoid death. He grew old, as would any man, but when came his time to die, he sprang a trap and captured Death. He bound Death in chains, so that Death could no longer claim any mortal. Zeus was forced to intervene.

"Sisyphus eventually arrived in Hades, but his wife, following his orders, had failed to give him a proper burial. Sisyphus was allowed to return to arrange for his remains to be properly disposed of. Once out of Hades, he refused to return, until Zeus once again intervened.

"As you can see, our good king is now condemned to struggle with that boulder till the end of time. No matter that he knows what will happen when he reaches the top, he cannot stop; a compulsion stronger than all human will forces him to try again, and again, and again."

Zac watched the scene play out, his fists clenched at his sides, his teeth gritted so hard his head hurt, willing Sisyphus to make it to the top of the hill, to win freedom from his torture. No crime imaginable deserved this kind of eternal punishment.

Inches from the crest of the hill, Sisyphus's knees buckled. With a heart-wrenching cry, he collapsed, and the boulder slipped from his grip, knocking him aside and rolling back to the base of the hill. He lay stunned only a moment; then the wild compulsion struck him again and he began crawling back down the hill on hands and knees.

"Let's move on," Ariadne said, leading a little farther down the path. A patch of light shone ahead, and she hurried toward it, seemingly eager to arrive at the next window to watch the suffering of another tortured soul.

Reaching the window himself, Zac attempted to pass beyond Ariadne without looking, but she grabbed his arm to stop him, as he knew she would.

"Take your medicine, like a good little boy," she said. "And remember, it would be most unwise to wander around Hades without a guide—you could end up doing more than just watching."

Zac turned to face the window. The sight that awaited him

was a man so emaciated he looked like a skeleton with dried-up skin clinging to it. Zac could see clearly the lines of his ribs, his jutting pelvic bones, his eyes, sunk deep into their sockets.

The man stood under a huge apple tree, its branches covered with emerald leaves surrounding abundant, shiny, red apples. The branches were so laden with ripe fruit that they sagged within the starving man's reach. His eyes gleamed as they fixed on one of those fruits. Slowly, as if trying to sneak up on it, he inched his hand toward the fruit, his eyes growing wider with hysterical hope as he got closer and closer. Then, as the tips of his fingers brushed the apple's skin, a gust of wind blew through the tree, boosting the branch high above the man's grasp. Feebly, he tried to jump on his brittle legs, but the wind steadily pushed the fruit beyond his reach. When he stopped reaching, the wind died, and the apple settled in front of his face.

"This is Tantalus," Ariadne said. "I'm sure you've heard of him."

On the far side of the apple tree, the gentle waves of a lake washed up on a smooth shore. Tantalus abandoned his efforts to pluck the apple from the tree, and gazed longingly at the clear, clean water.

"Tantalus was beloved of the gods," Ariadne continued. "He had their trust so completely that he ate at their table, sharing their nectar and ambrosia."

Tantalus had arrived at the shore of the lake now, the waves of crystal clear water washing up over his toes. Cupping his hand, he bent down toward the water.

"But Tantalus was guilty of that most terrible of crimes:

hubris. He thought he could fool the gods, and to do so he was willing to commit an atrocity. He murdered his own son, Pelops, and then cooked up the boy's body to serve as food for the gods."

As Tantalus's fingers were about to plunge into the water of the lake, the water suddenly receded, just far enough that he could not quite reach it. He took another step forward and reached out again, but once more, the water eluded him.

"You see how the gods have rewarded his crime," Ariadne said. "He will chase that water for miles, but never will he drink of it, and never will he pluck the tree's fruit."

"Why do I have to see this?" Zac asked, turning away from the window.

"You mean these fascinating scenes don't interest you?" Ariadne's eyes gleamed as she looked at him. "Well, there's no accounting for taste. But then, I think I know a little about where your tastes run, Hamlet dear. I'm sure this next scene will be much more to your liking."

The dread he thought he had left behind congealed in Zac's gut as Ariadne led him forward once again, toward another lighted window.

Carl parked his car in front of the Residence at 5:25. Cecile sat tensely beside him, wishing she could be anywhere but here.

"Are you sure you don't want me to wait for you?" Carl asked.

Cecile shook her head. "No, I'll be all right. I'll call you as soon as it's over." She could imagine what Mrs. Stanhope would think if she got a glimpse of Carl, with his ponytail and earring. At best, Carl would inspire raised eyebrows and questions about Cecile's moral fortitude.

"All right," he said. "I'll wait by the phone." He reached over and squeezed her knee, and it didn't occur to her until after he had withdrawn his hand that she should object.

She opened the car door and stepped out, waving weakly to Carl as he drove off, and then starting up the stairs, her legs trembling. It was dangerously close to 5:30, and Mrs. Stanhope was a stickler for punctuality.

The main hall of the Residence was usually deserted at this hour. One of the custodians was vacuuming the rug in front of the antique fireplace, but otherwise there was no one to be seen when Cecile stepped through the door. Then, a student emerged from the hallway that led to Mrs. Stanhope's office: Rose.

She was heading toward the stairs, probably on her way up to the headmistress's apartment, when she noticed Cecile approaching. She stopped with one foot on a step and one hand on the bannister, a self-satisfied smirk on her face as she stared at Cecile; then she turned and dashed up the stairs.

Cecile frowned, wondering if perhaps Rose had been looking out a window and had seen Carl. If she had, she was sure to tell her mother, no doubt with some extra embellishment.

Mrs. Stanhope didn't look up when Cecile stood in the doorway; she had a folder full of papers in front of her and was flipping through them, peering at them through the lenses of her half-glasses. Cecile saw that the folder had her name on it.

She rapped lightly on the door frame. Mrs. Stanhope

looked up, then pulled her glasses off and began piling the papers back into the folder. "Come in, Cecile," she said, her voice as warm as a January morning.

Nervously, Cecile chose one of the uncomfortable straight-backed chairs in front of Mrs. Stanhope's desk, placing her pocketbook with unnecessary care on the chair beside her. She felt like a student who had been sent to the principal's office.

Mrs. Stanhope rested her hands on the desk. "Have you given any thought to our earlier discussion?" she asked.

Cecile tamped down a surge of impatience and tried to answer calmly and reasonably. "Yes, of course I have. I'm afraid that my decision is final."

The corners of Mrs. Stanhope's mouth tugged down slightly. She leaned back in her chair and peered at Cecile. "Tell me, Cecile, are you reluctant to explain your reasons to me because you fear I might share this personal information with others?"

"Heavens no!" Cecile exclaimed, startled. It had never occurred to her that Mrs. Stanhope might take her refusal as a personal affront. "I have every faith in your discretion, Mrs. Stanhope."

"I'm glad. You know that any information you shared with me would be held in the strictest confidence?"

"Yes, I know that."

"Then I'm afraid I don't understand this reticence of yours. Surely you realize that it appears you're hiding something when you are so unwilling to talk to me."

Not if you had a modicum of trust in your fellow human beings, Cecile thought. This mean-spirited, nosy old busybody was trying to guilt-trip her into disclosing her reason for requesting a leave.

"I'm sorry if that's how it appears to you, Mrs. Stanhope. From where I sit, I'm merely protecting my own right to privacy."

Mrs. Stanhope's nostrils flared. "Privacy is all well and good, but we have a procedure to follow here, and you are refusing to follow it."

Cecile said nothing.

Mrs. Stanhope shook her head. "All right. I've given you every opportunity to be candid. I'm afraid I now must force the issue. Let me first assure you that what we say here is off the record. I have closed your file." She held her hands up as if to prove that she didn't have a weapon. Cecile was mystified by the sudden change of tone.

"You understand that you are a valuable member of the Walden community. Your students speak highly of you, and I myself have been impressed on those occasions when I have sat in on your classes. I am willing to make an exception to retain you on my staff. You may take the leave of absence you have requested."

"Thank you," Cecile said, her voice little more than a whisper. Mrs. Stanhope clearly had more to say, and something about the way she was couching her words so carefully filled Cecile with apprehension.

"All that said, however, let me make it quite plain that you had best use that time wisely and to your best advantage. If you have a 'problem,' take care of it while you're away. I want you well on the road to recovery when you return. And let me warn you: if this problem ever recurs, or if I ever hear of it manifesting itself on the grounds of this school, I will discharge you without hesitation. I am willing to give you a second chance, but you will not receive a third. Do I make myself clear?"

Cecile sat back in her chair and blinked. What on earth? "No, I'm afraid not. What do you mean? What 'problem?'"

Mrs. Stanhope stared piercingly, as if the force of her gaze could wrench Cecile's secret out of her. "Honesty would always best behoove you, Cecile, but I can understand that in this particular situation honesty is difficult."

"*What* situation? Mrs. Stanhope, I really don't know what you're accusing me of."

"I'm not accusing you of anything," Mrs. Stanhope said in her most soothing tones. "Let's just say it has come to my attention that some aspects of your behavior have been rather . . . erratic lately, and that given that information, your refusal to explain your request for a leave of absence leaves a certain impression."

Cecile remembered Rose's smirk, and realized exactly what Mrs. Stanhope was implying and who had led her to that conclusion. Indignation brought her to her feet. Mrs. Stanhope stood also, raising a placating hand as she did so, but nothing could hold back the burst of anger and hurt.

"You think I'm on drugs?!" Cecile shouted. Mrs. Stanhope opened her mouth to respond, but Cecile would not let her speak. "How dare you?" Tears brimmed in her eyes. "You got this from Rose, didn't you? She tells you some ridiculous story, and you instantly believe it when everyone but you knows what a liar she is!"

"You leave my daughter out of this!" Mrs. Stanhope

snapped, the color rushing to her face. "I am capable of reaching my own conclusions."

"So this is *your* conclusion? I don't want to reveal something very private that's happening in my life right now, and you decide that means I'm on drugs?" Cecile snatched up her pocketbook. "Was Rose by any chance in this office right before I got here? And is it possible that while she was here, *she* told you something that led you to believe that my behavior was—how did you put it—erratic?"

The color deepened on Mrs. Stanhope's cheeks.

"Maybe she said something as blatant as 'I saw Ms. Graham snorting cocaine in the bathroom.' Or more likely she came up with something decidedly more subtle, since even you would have a hard time believing that particular lie. Am I close?"

Mrs. Stanhope seemed near hyperventilating as Cecile stormed away from her and slammed the door on her way out, startling the poor custodian who had turned off the vacuum cleaner to dust the mantle.

Rushing for the exit, Cecile realized that her car was not in the parking lot. She would have to call Carl to come get her. She cursed out loud, then dashed down the stairs toward the teacher's lounge. The hallway leading to the lounge was dark and deserted, and she had to flick on the light switch to find her way. The lounge, too, was dark; even the light on the coffee maker was out. Cecile switched on two of the lamps, scrubbing tears from her burning eyes as she did so.

There was no going back now, she realized as she collapsed into the chair beside the phone. Mrs. Stanhope would never, ever forgive her for this outburst. What had happened to the calm, collected temperament she had always shown the world?

What were her chances of getting another teaching job after this? She couldn't use Walden as a reference—Mrs. Stanhope might go so far as to spread the rumor of Cecile's drug use, and that would be the most damning blow of all, never mind that there was no proof, and that the one who made the accusation was a spoiled teenager with a history of lying.

She picked up the phone, realizing that the enormity of what she had just done hadn't hit her yet. Carl answered on the first ring.

"I'm ready," she said, her voice no more than a whisper.

"I'm on my way," he told her. "What's wrong?"

"Just come get me."

She put the receiver back in the cradle and stared at the wall. Her eyes were dry now, and she felt no urge to cry. This had to be a momentary lull; even so, she was grateful for it. She was so tired of crying. Leaning her head back against the chair, she closed her eyes. How many times had she left a meeting with Mrs. Stanhope, fantasizing what she should have said? In the end, her words hadn't been as satisfying as she'd dreamed.

She was about to head out to the parking lot when she heard a click. She opened her eyes and saw only blackness. Great, she thought. She groped for the lamp beside her and turned the switch back and forth. Nothing. And not a dot of light from the outside reached into the teacher's lounge; she would have to make her way to the exit in darkness.

Taking up her pocketbook, she felt her way to the wall, stubbing her toe against the door to the lounge, but avoiding the other obstacles between her and the hallway. Once into the hall, she slid her feet carefully along the floor, knowing she had a clear route to the exit, except for a pair of steps about halfway there.

She had progressed only a few feet when she heard the sound of a footstep behind her. She froze, sudden fear clutching at her heart. The sound came again, a little closer this time. She strained her eyes in the blackness.

"Who's there?" she asked. There was no answer, but she sensed a presence. Someone *was* there, close by, silent. Her heart pounded as she slid her foot forward.

Instantly, she heard another footfall. She could not suppress a gasp. Then, she heard laughter. Soft, malicious, male laughter, very close.

Her knees went weak, and she almost collapsed, her heart leaping into her throat, cold sweat soaking her.

"I told you I wouldn't forget you, Precious." It was Steve's voice.

She screamed.

The laughter grew louder, closer. She bolted headlong into the darkness, the sound of Steve's footsteps loud in her ears. How far was the exit? How close was he?

She put her foot down on nothing. "The steps!" she thought, as she crashed to the ground, the impact knocking the last of the wind from her struggling lungs. Stunned, she lay on the floor, unable to draw breath, unable to move, as the footsteps behind her slowed to a stop inches away.

"You should watch where you're going, Precious. Looks like you took quite a nasty spill. I'll have to kiss it and make it better."

Cecile crawled away from the sound of his voice.

"Be still, my pet," he said. "I've been waiting for this moment for a very long time, you know."

Something brushed against her ribs, and Cecile squirmed away from the touch. A bit of air began seeping back into her chest now.

"That new boyfriend of yours has been a real pain in the ass," he continued, his hand trailing down her back. "I've had to work hard to get you alone. I sure hope he hasn't claimed the prize I've been waiting for so patiently."

Frantic, she tried to get more air into her lungs. If she could just catch her breath, she could stand up and run. Her knee ached terribly where she had banged it on the floor, but she could run on it. If it were shattered into a thousand pieces, she could run on it to escape Steve.

"I was hoping to take my time with you, but I suppose beggars can't be choosers, as the saying goes. I'll have to finish you off before your boyfriend takes it into his fool head to look for you down here."

Cecile felt him grab the hem of her skirt. With a desperate burst of energy, she surged to her feet, hearing Steve's curse as he reached for her and missed. Blindly, she blundered forward, running, caroming off the wall. Where was the exit? Had she, in her terror, turned the wrong way? She realized it didn't matter which way she went: either direction would get her out eventually, through the Residence or through the schoolhouse.

Muffling her breath, she stopped and leaned her back against the wall. She slid along, listening intently for the sound of Steve's feet, of his breathing, of his laughter. There was only silence, silence and the pounding of her heart. Where was he?

Her knee throbbed terribly, and each step sent shivers of pain up her leg. Any moment now, she expected to feel Steve's hand on her, to hear his laugh from inches away.

"You know, Precious, you're beginning to *annoy* me."

She froze. The echoes of the corridor made it hard to gauge where he was, or how close.

"I'll cut a deal with you," he said. "You make a little noise, tell me where you are, and I might be inclined to let you walk out of here when I'm finished with you."

Was the voice in front of her, or behind her? She couldn't tell, and not knowing, she dared not move. She pressed her back against the wall and stood still, like a frightened rabbit hoping against hope that the fox wouldn't see it.

"Come on, Precious. Quit playing hard to get." His voice sounded closer now. "You know you want me. Didn't you tell your little friends what a gorgeous hunk your mother was dating? Didn't you girls discuss your fantasies about me?"

Even in her terror, the blood rushed to Cecile's face. Did he actually *know* something? Had one of those girls revealed to Steve the school-girl crush Cecile had briefly had when she'd first met him? Surely not! And yet . . .

"Do you remember how you felt when you saw me fucking that bimbo?"

Steve's voice seemed to be everywhere, one moment to her left, the next, to her right. Was it the echoes in the corridor? Or was fear muddling her senses?

"Why did you stand and watch? Have you asked yourself that? Why didn't you just turn tail and run? Did you maybe wish it were you?"

No! Cecile thought to herself, biting down hard on her tongue to keep from screaming it aloud.

"Have you been saving yourself ever since? Waiting for the day I would find you again?"

Suddenly, a hand grabbed Cecile's upper arm, hard.

"No!" she screamed, all her terror coming out in that one word. She tore away and turned and fled down the corridor, not caring which way she was going, running until she stumbled into something soft and warm. She screamed once again as arms wrapped around her, trapping her. She thrashed and fought and screamed, hoping someone would hear and rescue her. Then, she had to pause to draw a breath.

"Cecile! Stop it, it's me!"

It was Carl's voice. "Carl! Oh, thank God!" she said, the words coming out a frantic sob. "He's here! He's here!"

"Shh," Carl said, one hand stroking her hair while the other pinned her firmly against his chest. "You're safe now. Come on, the stairs are this way. Just hold on to me."

They were moving, slowly, cautiously, when the lights went on. Carl quickly glanced up and down the corridor, retaining his hold on Cecile. "There's no one there, sweetheart," he said.

She wrenched herself out of his arms to see for herself. The corridor was empty. "He must have gone back to the schoolhouse," she said.

Carl took her in his arms once more. She buried her head against his chest and returned his embrace. "Carl, you saved my life," she murmured.

His arms tightened around her, his hands rubbing her

back, kneading the tense muscles at the base of her neck. "It was Steve?" he asked. "Did you see him?"

"I heard him. And I felt him. He attacked me."

"It's a good thing I came inside. You sounded so terrible on the phone I decided you were past caring whether you were seen with me or not."

"Carl, I don't know how to thank you. I—"

"Shh," he said, pulling away and putting his finger to her lips.

Cecile met his eyes, forgetting to brace herself for the jolt she always felt when she did so. Her pulse pounded—had it slowed at all yet? Carl gazed at her, his eyes intense, burning, demanding. Almost against her will, she kissed the finger he held poised against her lips. He leaned in on her, not blinking, not even breathing. A part of her shouted a warning, but she ignored it, parting her lips to receive his kiss.

She half-expected him to withdraw, but this time, he did not. His lips brushed hers, and a soft gasp escaped her. That kiss seemed to burn, and the fire traveled from her lips downward. He pulled away for just an instant, then pressed his mouth against hers so hard it hurt.

Cecile held him tight against her, clinging to him as he pushed her backward against the wall. The fire burned so brightly she could not resist it, and even when Carl pulled away, she found herself leaning toward him, grabbing him and pressing herself against him, needing to feel his hands on her body.

Carl bent his head to her ear. "Does this mean 'yes?'" he asked in a hoarse whisper.

"Yes."

10

Tears dribbled down Cecile's cheeks, soaking the pillow on which she rested. The heat of Carl's body was slowly fading. She listened to him dress, muffling her sniffles, clenching her fists, trying to keep her quiet tears from becoming wrenching sobs. He said nothing, offered no consolation or comfort. She heard only his footsteps as he left the room, closing the door behind him.

She sat up in the bed, staring at the door, clutching a sheet against her naked chest and shivering as she tried to fight down the waves of remorse. When was the last time she'd had any control over her life? Or over herself? It seemed impossibly long ago.

She wanted to believe that the chill in Carl's demeanor was imagined, that he would return to the room, offering once more his warmth and protection. And yet . . . something had changed. She felt it, as surely as she felt the pain from her bruises and the throbbing of her knee.

Carl flung the door open suddenly, letting in the brightness from the living room. She gasped and shielded her eyes, holding the blankets closer to her chest as he approached. He placed a steaming cup on the nightstand beside her.

"Drink up," he said, when she made no move to reach for it. No hint of warmth in his words.

Cecile picked up the cup and took a sip, scalding her tongue. The tea was strong and bitter.

Sitting down in the corner chair, Carl propped up his legs on the nightstand. "So, was it worth it?"

She could feel his gaze upon her, but could not bring herself to look at him. "What do you mean?" she whispered.

"The price you paid for protection. Was it worth it?"

Cecile looked up then. He was grinning at her, a twisted, mean-spirited grin to go with his words.

"That's why you did it, isn't it?" he continued casually, still grinning. "You realized shortly after we got into bed that you didn't *really* mean yes, didn't you? But you never told me to stop. Why is that?"

Of course he had known she didn't want to do it! How could he not have sensed the tension in her? "You could have stopped, if you realized I didn't want to," she said.

"Why should I stop? I was getting what I wanted. And you got what you wanted. You didn't dare ask me to stop, because you were afraid I wouldn't stick around to protect you if you did."

Cecile winced, wondering if he would abandon her anyway, then wondering if she would be better off if he did. "Would you have stopped if I'd asked?"

He laughed. "I'll leave that to your imagination, my dear, which seems to be quite vivid these days."

"What do you mean? If you're implying that I *imagined*

Steve was there tonight—" She thrust her arm at him. "Do you think I imagined these?"

Carl glanced briefly at her arm, where dark bruises were beginning to appear. He shook his head. "Far from it," he said. "Actually, this all has very little to do with *your* imagination."

"Meaning what?"

The phone rang, its sound so sudden that Cecile jumped. Letting his enigmatic statement hang unexplained, Carl picked up the receiver.

"Hello," he said, then listened for a while. "As luck would have it, she's right here." He handed the phone to Cecile, who stared at it dumbly. "It's Robbins," he said. "He was just calling to see if I knew where you could be reached."

Cecile took the phone. "Hello," she said.

"Hello, Ms. Graham," the detective's familiar voice said. "Just getting back to you about your stepfather's whereabouts. We checked up on him, and he's in Texas."

Cecile shook her head. "That's impossible! I know he's here!"

"According to his employer, he hasn't taken any time off recently. So he couldn't be the one who left the note you showed us."

"But . . . but . . . " Cecile couldn't get her mouth around the protest she wanted to utter.

"I'm sorry, ma'am, there's not much more we can do."

"You don't understand," Cecile wailed. "I *know* he's not in Texas!"

"Yes, ma'am, he is," the detective said, his voice betraying a hint of impatience.

"He was at the Walden school! This evening!"

"You've seen him? Are you positive?"

Cecile sighed in exasperation. "I didn't exactly see him, but . . ." Her voice trailed off.

"Well, until you exactly see him, I'm going to have to assume that his boss is telling us the truth and that he has been at work. In Texas."

Had his boss lied for him? She mumbled a thank you, then hung up the phone, shaking her head. "I don't understand," she whispered.

"Don't you?" Carl asked. He swung his legs off the nightstand and stood up, his grin turning from malicious to savage. She quailed before him even as she found herself transfixed by his eyes, unable to move, unable to look away.

"I have not forgotten you," he whispered.

Cecile's blood ran cold.

"You know you want me," he said, Steve's voice somehow emanating from his lips.

"No!" Cecile screamed. She tried to spring out of the bed, willing to run naked into the street if necessary, but Carl grabbed her shoulders and flung her back onto the bed, his body landing on top of hers, pinning her down as his hand clamped over her mouth.

"Be still, Cecile," he said. "This is not over yet. I have a few more confidences to share with you."

She struggled, trying to throw him off, but he was too strong.

"Poor little fool," he said, his hand sliding from her mouth to her hair as he held her pinned. "It took so little to make you believe."

"It was you in the hallway."

"Yes."

"And you left the bottle of Scotch at Zac's."

"Yes. And? What else?"

She shook her head, pain sucking the air from her lungs.

"What else, Cecile?" Carl urged, pressing down on her even harder. "What else has 'Steve' done?"

Tears dribbled out of her closed eyes. "You killed Bess."

He laughed. "Yes. She was beginning to make a nuisance of herself. But, you might wonder, how did I manage it? I was with you when it happened, wasn't I?"

It was true. He *had* been with her.

"Who are you?" Cecile cried.

"An interesting question; I'm not sure how to answer it." He looked momentarily pensive. "Far more revealing, is *what* I am."

Cecile said nothing, her eyes squeezed shut as if that could block him out of her life. Carl wound a hand in her hair and pulled. She gasped in pain.

"Ask me!" he insisted.

"What . . . are you?"

"I'll show you," he said.

Dizziness overwhelmed her, and blackness descended.

Ariadne beckoned with her index finger, and Zac came forward, his heart fluttering in his chest as he approached the third lighted window. It was too late for second thoughts. If he had followed her this far in error, then his soul was already lost.

He glanced in the window and saw a beautiful girl, maybe

fourteen or fifteen years old. Lustrous, curly black hair surrounded her round, olive-skinned face. She wore a short white tunic that showed off her legs as she wandered through a meadow of wildflowers in the midst of a thick copse of woods.

"Her name is Eliana," Ariadne said. "She's a nobleman's daughter, and she has lived a protected life. Her father has shielded her from the harsher realities of the world so that she can go to her eventual marriage a true innocent."

The girl picked a daisy and tucked it behind her ear, then picked another and laughingly tucked it down the front of her tunic, into her cleavage.

"She's in a playful mood today," Ariadne went on. "She's managed to slip away from home on her own for once, and she's enjoying her freedom. She's looking for a pond that she knows is around here somewhere, so she can have a delightfully wicked swim. In life, she found that pond and had her swim; then, she returned home to a severe scolding from her offended father.

"Eliana went on to marry well, as her father had wished. She went to her wedding bed a virgin, ignorant of the ways of physical love, which her husband introduced her to slowly and gently, to her great satisfaction. Later, she found that satisfaction too much to resist. So, when her husband was away at war, she sampled several of his friends. There was one, however, who refused her advances. His name was Caramos, and because he was the only one to refuse her, he was the only one she truly wanted.

"When her husband returned, Eliana was with child. She had no wish to taste her husband's temper, and told him she'd been raped, naming Caramos as the unborn child's father. Eliana was present on the day that poor, innocent man was gelded on her accusation.

"But that was in life. In death, her destiny is quite different."

Eliana looked up from picking her flowers. A man had emerged from the woods ahead of her, and she raised her hand to wave at him.

"That is Caramos, in the prime of his youth," Ariadne said.

Eliana seemed to know him, and carried on a shouted conversation, punctuated by giggles. Caramos laughed as he came closer, showing every sign of being harmless and friendly.

Movement at the edge of the woods behind the girl caught Zac's eye. Caramos was not alone; three other men had emerged from the woods, fanning out stealthily and cutting off any avenue of escape as they closed in on the girl, who was too distracted by Caramos to notice them.

Ariadne pressed her body against Zac's back and wrapped her arms around his chest. "Guess what's going to happen to her, Hamlet," she whispered.

One of the stalking men must have made a noise, for suddenly Eliana looked behind her. She was too naive to be instantly alarmed at seeing the three of them advancing on her. Her face registered only puzzlement. Then, Caramos reached out and pulled up the bottom of her tunic. She shrieked and whirled around to face him.

The tip of Ariadne's tongue touched Zac's earlobe and her hand moved downward over his chest and belly. Zac willed himself to pull away from her, to turn his head from the scene in the meadow, but he could not. His breath came shallow, and a strange sensation like the flutter of butterfly wings traveled from his chest, to his gut, to his groin.

Eliana realized her danger now. One of the men grabbed her around the waist, pinning her arms at her sides. Eliana struggled, kicking wildly at Caramos as he tore away her tunic. He batted away her kick with his forearm and picked up the daisy that had fallen from her cleavage, using it to tickle her nipples, and to brush at her tears.

"Just imagine what that kind of power must be like," Ariadne whispered in Zac's ear. "He can do anything he wants to her. She can fight, and kick, and scream, but in the end, she is helpless before him. How heady that must be, no?"

Zac's breath choked him as he tried to muster a denial while lust coursed through his veins and throbbed in his temples.

"Would you like to take me now?" Ariadne asked.

"No," he managed to force out.

Caramos plucked off the petals of the daisy one by one and blew them into Eliana's terror-stricken face. He then barked an order at his men, and they wrestled her easily to the ground, one of them pinning her arms above her head, while the others each took hold of one of her legs and pulled them wide apart. Caramos stood between her legs and laughed at her pointless struggles.

Tears burned in Zac's eyes even as his desire flared higher and higher. No, he kept repeating to himself. No, this scene was not exciting him. No, he was not a monster. No, whatever it was that caused this physical reaction in him was not real, was not *him*.

"What's the matter, Hamlet? Isn't this deep down one of your greatest fantasies, being played out before your very eyes? Haven't you always wanted to—"

"No!" Zac roared, but still he could not pull away and could not turn his head.

Caramos had disrobed now. Savagely, he flung himself on top of Eliana. Her piercing scream told Zac when Caramos penetrated her. The screams continued, but soon lost strength and turned to sobs as Caramos heaved on top of her. Eventually, his men were sure enough of her defeat to release her arms and legs. She offered no further resistance.

"The others will take turns with her when Caramos is finished," Ariadne said, her hand sliding slowly, steadily downward. "And then, when it's all over, she'll be walking innocently through the field again, picking daisies, ready to have her virginity torn from her once more."

Zac moaned as her hand massaged him. This was more than he could bear, this Other Zac who was taking pleasure from the brutal rape of a young girl.

"Do you want to fuck me, Hamlet? I know you do. *You* know you do. Why fight it? You've reached the end; now, let it happen."

Yes, the Other Zac thought. Why shouldn't he? What did it matter, anyway? This wasn't real. And Ariadne was no innocent virgin. Why, he had had her many times already! It was time to accept his own feelings, accept them and act on them.

Ariadne rubbed her entire body against him as she slid under his arm to face him. He reached behind her and grabbed the neck of her robe with both hands, then jerked with all his strength. The robe tore easily, baring her skin to him. She pressed her mouth against his chest as the remnants of the robe fell to the ground. His skin tingled and burned where Ariadne's body pressed against it. He wanted her. He *must* have her!

A dark mist descended over his eyes as his hands found her breasts. Blood roared in his ears, and above the roaring he heard Eliana resume her screams. He tried to lower Ariadne to the ground, but she resisted, twisting out of his hands. "No!" she shouted, but he reached for her again, catching her upper arm, clenching tightly upon her.

"No!" he heard Eliana scream in the background. His eyes flitted in her direction, but the light in the window had dimmed.

Ariadne slammed the heel of her hand into Zac's chest. He bellowed in pain, and his hand flew out, of its own accord, catching the side of her face. He heard her cry out as she fell to the ground, and as his head spun with a giddy rush, desire engulfed him completely. He flung himself on top of her, feeling her squirm and writhe beneath him, screams filling the air around him. She kicked and scratched and struggled, but an inhuman strength was upon him, and she could not throw him off. He jammed his knee down hard on the soft flesh between her thighs, forcing them apart.

"Please!" she wailed, and no word or sound could have inflamed him more. For all her mockery, for all the anguish she had brought him, he wanted to hear *her* beg; to have her for once at *his* mercy, asking *him* to stop; to watch *her* humiliation, knowing he had the power to stop it. And to choose not to.

"Yes!" he cried in exhilaration as he sank into her. The mist enshrouded his mind, and he knew no more.

He was lying on his back, staring into the black sky of Hades. His breaths came in gasps, and his body was soaked in sweat, quickly cooling. Every muscle in Zac's body felt heavy and weak, sated completely. He wanted to close his eyes and drift into blissful sleep. But something disturbed him. A sound. A sound that was not right, that intruded on his tranquility. Then he recognized that sound: sobbing. Someone was crying, whether Ariadne or Eliana, he didn't know.

But why should he think it was Ariadne? Surely she had been in full control of the situation, had goaded him into his brutality. When would he learn that her control was absolute?

She had wanted him to do it! Why else would she make him watch the scene in the meadow, then try to seduce him, then refuse him once he had started? She had screamed and fought only to prove to him that she was right, that the power of that act was intoxicating to him at some base level that he didn't want to admit to. Shouldn't she be gloating now?

But then, the sobs were too close to be Eliana's; it had to be Ariadne. He dared not look at her, but stared into the darkness, as his heart calmed and doubt wormed its way into his head.

Then, he heard the sound he had been expecting: Ariadne's laughter.

And yet, the sobbing continued.

Ariadne approached from his right side, the side away from the crying. Victory shone in her smile as she stood over him. She was fully clothed.

"Turn your head, Hamlet," she said.

Fear seized him by the throat. It was not Eliana who was crying, for he could even now hear her begin to talk with Caramos as he entered the meadow.

"You don't dare look, do you?" she said. "Do you know why? It's because you know in your heart what you will find when you turn your head. You knew all along."

"No," he whispered, his throat collapsing on itself, on his voice, on his breath.

"Then look, Zac."

He could not.

"If you haven't the courage, I'll help you." She stepped over him. Zac heard a sudden shriek, and his body went rigid. His heart seemed to stop as Ariadne dragged his victim from the darkness. A massive bruise covered one side of her face, and her eyes were swollen almost shut from crying, but nothing could hide from Zac the horror of his realization: it was Cecile.

Ariadne held Cecile's battered face before him, then flung her into the surrounding darkness. He wrenched himself into a sitting position, reaching out to the darkness where she had disappeared.

"Don't bother," Ariadne said. "She has served her purpose, and I have sent her away. Tell me, was it as satisfying as you always dreamed it would be?"

Zac's heart beat erratically, and his head spun. He had *not* hurt Cecile. It had been Ariadne all along, and Cecile was but an illusion, a dream. "It wasn't real," he whispered.

"It was, and you knew it was. I took the illusion of my face from her, long before it was too late. You knew what you were doing; why else would you have felt that sense of dread when it was over?"

He *had* felt it. But it was impossible to imagine that he could have done such a thing to Cecile. It was impossible.

"A part of you has been wanting to do this to her since the first time she refused you." Zac opened his mouth, but she interrupted before he could speak. "Don't start an argument you can't win. I've seen what you're capable of! You can tell yourself over and over that I goaded you into it, but you know you wanted this. Now, Cecile knows it too."

Zac felt a scream building in his gut, rising, lodging firmly in his chest. "Why?" he managed to gasp.

Suddenly, the whole world was revolving about him with incredible speed. Glaring white light blinded him, burning his skin, sending spikes of pain to the back of his head.

Finally, the pain receded, and Zac was sitting on a cold, featureless white floor, looking at image upon image of himself. He turned his head right and left, but saw only himself, reflected on the surface of hundreds upon hundreds of mirrors.

Then, Ariadne appeared beside him in each of those mirrors. He focused on one of her reflections, finding it easier to gaze upon than his own.

"Look at yourself, Zac. Look and see what you will have to face, every time you look into a mirror, and every time you look into Cecile's eyes, for the rest of your life."

He looked at his reflection. His eyes were sunken and

haunted, and the horror of his own actions was etched in his face.

The scene in the mirror shifted. Zac saw himself running down a narrow corridor, screaming and bumping into walls. He was in the Labyrinth of Crete, running like a coward from the pursuing Minotaur. The scene shifted again, and he saw himself in the cabin with Ariadne. She was astride him, her head thrown back, her back arched with her efforts, while his face was frozen in pleasure. Once more, the image shifted, showing him punching Ariadne in the face, showing the blood that trickled from the corner of her mouth.

Then he saw himself on top of Cecile, her mouth open in a silent scream as he forced himself on her like an animal.

He turned away. He could not watch this, could not see it.

"How unfortunate for you that you have a conscience," Ariadne said. "I, for one, have none, and such torments as you suffer would not trouble me in the least."

He looked up once more. The mirror before him now reflected only himself and Ariadne. "Who are you?" he asked, his heart answering his question even as the words left his mouth.

Ariadne feigned surprise. "You don't know? You remember what I told you, don't you? Carcajou is a prism who casts many reflections. I am one of them." Her image in the mirror changed suddenly, becoming the evil monk Zac had encountered at the monkey temple. Turning his head, Zac saw a different figure reflected in another mirror: the Minotaur. Another mirror showed a figure he did not recognize: a tall, sharp-featured man with long dark hair pulled back into a ponytail. Ariadne appeared in yet another mirror, and Zac fixed his eyes on that image.

His mind couldn't quite encompass the idea, though he was certain she was telling the truth for once. "You've been leading me here," he whispered.

"Yes. I told you early on that Carcajou wanted you to stay here."

"But you never said why."

"As you may have guessed, this world that you have so rudely invaded is my personal domain—No!" she said, raising her hand as Zac started to protest. "You were always welcome to visit. In fact, you were more than welcome. You are my bridge into your world. Obviously, it behooves me to keep you here.

"While you were visiting my world, I had a chance to take a look at yours. I liked what I saw. You've heard it said: Alexander wept when he saw he had no more worlds to conquer. I have never been one to weep, myself.

"I was willing to take my time, to learn and to explore. But you fell in love! You stopped coming. My bridge was lost. Or so it seemed, until I discovered that *I* could initiate your journeys. And that I was better at it than you.

"I've learned a great deal while you've been in my labyrinth, and I've grown stronger. I can now send multiple reflections into your world."

"Why did you . . . put me through this hell?"

Her image in the mirror shimmered, several of her other reflections flickering past. Then the image solidified once more. "To keep you here by force, I must concentrate much of my will on you alone. I much prefer the freedom to focus my energy on exploring your world and expanding my powers there. Thus, I had to convince you to stay of your own free will."

Zac stared at her, and laughter built in his chest. "Oh, yes, I can see that's what you've been trying to do," he said as the laughter bubbled out of him, uncontrolled, verging on hysteria. "Sure, I'll stay. I'll happily stay. Who wouldn't want to live in this paradise, especially with you for company?"

Ariadne sneered. "You don't even begin to understand! Think for a moment what you have to go back to now. Remember how you felt when you looked at yourself in the mirror."

The sobering thought halted Zac's laughter.

"You will not shake your memories. I've made sure of that. Can you feel the self-loathing even now, eating away at you?"

"Yes," he admitted, "but—"

"I haven't finished." The image in the mirror flickered once more, this time resolving itself into the figure of the dark man that Zac had not recognized. "You've forgotten about the little forays I've been making into your world," he said.

Zac stared at the sharp-featured man and realized who he must be.

"Yes, I'm the one who's been . . . 'comforting' Cecile in your absence. Or should I say, 'fucking' her."

"Bastard!"

"She has you to thank for all of this, Zac."

Zac stared at the floor, shaking his head.

"You're supposed to bleat out 'Why?' again," Carcajou said. "I feared you might decide you could live with yourself, in spite of it all. It therefore became necessary to provide an additional form of persuasion. Can you also live with the knowledge that Cecile has seen your true self? That her face will forever haunt you, even as you try in vain to shake your memories of this place, of the brutal rape you put her through? You'll never be free." Carcajou's eyes pierced him, knowing him to his very core; knowing that his victory was absolute.

Zac looked up. "What is it you want of me?" he whispered.

"I have risked everything, gambled my considerable hold on you to bring you to this point." As he said those words, his eyes seemed to glow. A charged tension crackled between Zac and each of the many mirrors. "You can return to your own world and live out your miserable existence. But, I offer you an alternative. I can free you from the torments I've inflicted upon you.

"I can wipe your memory clean of all that has happened here. You will have your own part of the labyrinth. You will find Cecile there. Or at least, someone who will seem like Cecile, before she encountered me, before she knew anything about your secret life. The illusion will be absolute, and you will be free."

Zac's heart ached. Moments ago he had thought that his only freedom lay in death; and he had found himself welcoming that eventuality.

"And while I'm here, you are free to do whatever you want in my world?" Zac asked.

"That is the bargain you strike."

"What happens to Cecile?"

"You will have the Cecile you always wanted. My Cecile

will no longer concern you."

His Cecile? Did he mean he would continue to torment her? "You must free Cecile also," Zac said.

Carcajou laughed. "You have no bargaining power, my friend."

"I think I do. Otherwise, we wouldn't be here."

"I grow impatient. Very well, if it pleases you, I will leave Cecile to herself."

"So you say."

"With access to your whole world, why would I waste my time on one inconsequential woman? I have made you an offer. Now it is for you to take it. Or leave it, if you prefer."

Zac yearned for nothing more than complete oblivion. But would he be leaving Cecile at Carcajou's mercy?

"You're afraid of feeling guilty," Carcajou said. "Keep in mind that when you forget, you will forget all."

"How do I know you're telling the truth? You've lied—"

"But always with a purpose. I do not lie for the sake of lying. Nor did I ever torment you for the sake of tormenting you. My purpose was to lead you to this moment, this decision."

"And Cecile? Why did you torment her?"

"For the same reason: to lead you to this moment. If you choose to return to your world, surely Cecile's heart will be forever lost to you. Would she let you ease her pain, knowing it was you who brought that pain upon her? Could you bear the burden of your guilt?"

The image shifted again, taking on Ariadne's features once more. "My poor Hamlet," she said. "Choosing has never been one of your strong suits."

"What if I refuse to make a choice?"

Ariadne snorted. "Resolute in your indecision to the last! I will be displeased, of course. You will forget nothing. I will make your life miserable, and Cecile's as well. Perhaps I would even find it necessary to kill Cecile. I considered doing so once—knowing you might retreat to my domain more often than ever—but feared you would take your own life."

Zac looked into the mirror that held his own face beside Ariadne's, into his own eyes, and saw the Other Zac reflected there, ready to wholly subsume the man he once was. The guilt would last only as long as it took him to say "I accept."

And yet, who could Cecile turn to, if Carcajou didn't release her?

"The time has come. Decide."

Sick at heart, his stomach clenching, Zac looked away from himself, at Ariadne. His body shook with the conflict that engulfed him.

"Spit it out, Hamlet. Let's have done with this."

"No." The sound that somehow forced its way past his lips startled him.

Ariadne frowned. "You try my patience. Make your decision."

"No." His heart beat harder against his chest, the strain of speaking that single word sucking all the strength out of him.

"You must decide. You know that."

Zac shook his head. It was easier than talking, but he knew he had to speak. "Send me back," he croaked, and felt his heart would explode with the thought of it.

Ariadne's eyes widened with genuine shock.

Zac sucked in a breath. Electricity sizzled over his skin and every hair on his body stood up. "You heard me," he said. "Send me back." The disbelief he saw in her face was almost comical.

"You reject my offer?"

"Yes."

"You *are* a fool!"

"Maybe so. But send me back." Perhaps there was no way he could have known or guessed that Ariadne was the enemy. He had followed her to the heart of Carcajou's labyrinth, convinced he had no choice. But in the end, there *was* a choice.

And this time, he would make the right one.

He faced Ariadne again. "It would be easy to come here one last time, to hide from the world forever. But I won't leave Cecile alone to face you and whatever demons you've awakened in her. Send me back."

She laughed, but it was a tense laughter, and Zac could feel her grip on him slipping. "I thought you had more sense in that skull of yours," she said. "Do you really think she will have anything to do with you, knowing what you've become, what you are?"

"It doesn't matter. I'll be there if she needs me. And even if I never see her again, maybe she'll take some comfort in knowing there's someone in the world who understands."

Ariadne's face hardened, her expression unfathomable. Zac waited for the anger, for the explosion. She was absolute ruler of her world.

The rage did not come. He could sense it, bubbling beneath her skin, but it did not come. "Very well," she said, her voice tightly controlled. "Go back. I'm sure a happy life awaits you, as a reward for your gallantry."

Her face warped before him, her cruel smile becoming the Minotaur's toothy snarl. She spoke, her voice dripping with hatred: "The game isn't quite over, Hamlet. We'll see who wins in the last moments." A malignant gleam appeared in her eyes, and Zac was overcome with dizziness.

11

Cecile's clothes clung to her body, wet with the sweat of her fear. Her heart still hammered in her chest, and tears burned her eyes. She blinked, and looked around her.

She was in what looked to be a private hospital room, obviously belonging to a wealthy patient. There were homey touches to the room: an oriental rug upon which the hospital bed sat, and a plush sofa on which Cecile found herself lying.

"Did you have a nice nap?" She jumped upright. Carl was seated beside her on the sofa. "I thought after your adventures you might like to visit with your dear lover."

Cecile stood up. Yes, that was Zac lying on the bed. Even from across the room, she could see his eyeballs racing under his lids, his limbs twitching erratically under the sheet. She stepped to the side of the bed and gripped the railing. She was aware of Carl moving with her, coming close enough behind her that she could feel the warmth of his body.

"He's not quite the saint you thought he was, is he?" Carl whispered in her ear.

"That wasn't him," she said. "I know him. It's just an

illusion, one of your many, apparently."

"Yes, tell yourself that," he crooned. "It's easier to bear than the truth, I'm sure. And yet, you thought you knew *yourself*, didn't you? Did you ever imagine yourself fucking your new neighbor while the love of your life lay in a coma?"

Tears dribbled down Cecile's face as she looked down at Zac. His cheeks were gaunt, his body frail and vulnerable as he lay before her. What must Carl have done to him to turn such a sweet-natured, gentle man into the creature she had seen?

"Imagine what he's going through right now," Carl said. "He's not just dreaming it, as you once must have thought. He is living it, his every sense awake to it. He is truly in Hell."

"Shut up!" Cecile cried, the tears coming harder.

Carl grabbed her shoulders and spun her around to face him. She quickly looked away, but he took hold of her chin and wrenched it upward, forcing her to meet his eyes. Glimmers of silver light danced behind his black pupils and her breath seemed to stop in her throat as his eyes engulfed her.

"You can free him, Cecile," he said. "You have the power."

"What do you want?"

He let go of her chin. Stepping over to an equipment chest in the corner of the room, he opened a drawer and withdrew a needle and syringe. From another compartment he removed a small vial of clear liquid. Cecile watched as he filled the syringe, then brought it to her. She backed away from him, her eyes darting around the room, looking for something with which to ward him off.

Carl laughed. "The needle's not for you, my sweet. If I'd

wanted to kill you, I would have done so while you slept. It's for him." He nodded toward Zac.

Cecile maneuvered a chair between herself and Carl. Was there anyone else in this building? She screamed, as loud as she could.

Carl shook his head at her. "That won't work," he assured her. "Everyone in this house has 'mysteriously' fallen asleep. Yes, you're in his brother's house." He moved in closer to her, the needle pointed upward.

She kept the chair between them, watching him warily, waiting for him to pounce. And he did, more suddenly than she could have anticipated. He darted forward and with the back of his free hand slammed the chair out of the way with such force that its wooden back shattered when it hit the wall. Cecile leapt backward, but the wall was behind her, and Carl was before her, advancing.

"Come now, Cecile. It's time to end this game." He held the needle out to her. "You can free Zac from my world, and free yourself at the same time. All you have to do is take this needle and deliver its contents into his arm. What could be easier?"

"Get away from me."

"I'm not going to go away, my dear. You must know that by now. Take this." He thrust the needle toward her. She stared at it in mute horror. "Take it!" he ordered, more sharply.

She took the needle from his outstretched hand, and he backed off, leaving her a clear pathway to Zac's bed.

"There's a good girl," he said. "Now, go on and give it to Zac."

She stared at Zac's body, twitching on the bed.

Carl said, "The only release he will ever find is in death. And that, you can bring to him with your own loving hand."

She shook her head violently. "I won't!"

"No? After what he did to you? You don't think a man like that deserves to die?"

"No!" she said, but her hand trembled as the memories flooded through her. He was so different from Steve, so gentle. And yet . . . he had been merciless.

"Touching. You forgive him for raping you. But if you won't take his life in revenge, will you take it out of compassion? Does he deserve this living hell?"

"Shut up."

"Because that's what he will endure for the rest of his life. That is what you condemn him to."

Cecile moved over to the bed. As she looked down at Zac's face, Carl lowered the guardrail. She sat on the bed, the needle in her right hand as she brushed Zac's hair away from his eyes with her left. How forlorn and powerless he looked. Was Carl right? Did she in fact condemn Zac by refusing to end his torment?

Her heart ached terribly, and she wondered if she shouldn't use the needle on herself. She had long known that Steve would haunt her the rest of her days; she knew now that she would never be free of her present-day ghosts either.

"Go on," Carl said. "End it. If you want, there's plenty in that needle for you, too."

She turned to him. "If you want him dead so badly, why don't *you* do it?"

"Because I want you to do it." He hovered over her with

a hint of a grin on his face. "Wouldn't he prefer to die by your loving hand than by mine?"

"I can't," she said, placing the needle on the bed.

"Kill him, and I lose my doorway. Your world will be free of me."

She shook her head. "I can't do it." She reached out and touched Zac's face again. Sorrow pressed on her like a heavy blanket, leaving the air stale and sluggish.

Carl picked up the needle. Cecile watched numbly as he lifted Zac's arm and prepared to inject the drug. She knew she could do nothing to stop him from killing both of them, if he wanted to. She didn't have the strength. But if that was the case . . .

"Wait," she whispered, as the needle touched Zac's skin. She reached for Carl's arm, afraid to grab on lest he reflexively push the drug in.

He grinned at her and withdrew the needle. "You've changed your mind?"

"Yes," she said. "He'd rather I did it."

"Be my guest." His eyes burned into her, seeing deep inside her, as she took the needle from him. Her hands shook, and her head throbbed with pain, as if his eyes were penetrating her mind, searching out the last of her secrets.

She bent over Zac, kissed his forehead. "Goodbye, my love," she said, choking back her tears. She felt Carl's breath on her neck as he leaned over her, watching eagerly. She reached for Zac's arm. Her grip tightened on the syringe and she whipped around with all the quickness she could muster, her hand flying blindly toward Carl's body. She felt the needle make contact, and she shoved in the plunger, sinking all the drug she could into whatever part of Carl's body she had found.

Carl let out a hideous, bestial roar as he surged away from her, one flailing hand catching her in the ribs. A wall of pain slammed into her, and she collapsed on the floor, clutching at her middle, the empty syringe still in her hand. Through eyes almost closed with pain, she saw Carl grab a rolling tray from against the wall and lift it over his head, slamming it to the ground with a deafening crash. He howled again, then kicked out at the bed on which Zac lay. The leg of the bed crumbled with the force of the kick, sending Zac sprawling onto the floor.

Cecile crawled toward Zac's inert body. Every labored breath stabbed at her lungs, but she was able to lay a hand on Zac, to feel his heartbeat, as Carl's fury methodically destroyed the room. She lay across Zac's body, shielding him from the flying debris, waiting for Carl to turn his wrath on them.

Eventually Carl's bellowing ceased, and Cecile risked a glance upward, hoping to see his body collapsed on the floor. Instead, she met his hate-filled eyes as he towered over her. "Go ahead and kill us, if you're going to," she told him. The words sent slicing pains through her chest, but she was surprisingly unafraid. The terror of death had lost its hold over her.

Carl shook his head. "It was a surprise to learn that I had misjudged one of you. To have misjudged you both is unthinkable. It is a mistake I will not make again, should I find another doorway to this world." His voice showed no hint of the venomous anger that flashed in his eyes.

Zac groaned and moved. Cecile's heart leapt with hope, but she dared not take her eyes off of Carl.

"He's waking," Carl said. "I'll let him. I'll let you live too, dearest Cecile. But, in the end, I'm not at all sure you will thank me for that consideration."

Zac groaned again, and Carl's body flickered suddenly, like an image from a movie projector. He flickered once more, becoming suddenly translucent and insubstantial. "Till we meet again," he said, and his image vanished.

Cecile rolled off of Zac. As she watched, he awakened, and met her eyes. His own eyes widened, then winced in pain. He covered his face with his hands and wept, great racking sobs that shook his entire body.

Cecile hung her head and wondered what the future would bring.

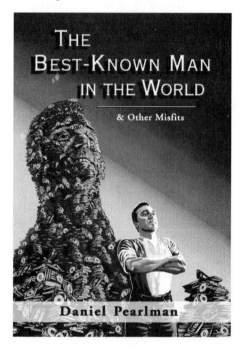

Jennifer Barlow graduated from Duke University with a degree in physical anthropology. She has since put that degree to good use as a dog groomer, a test scorer, and a technical writer. A native of Philadelphia, she now resides in Durham, North Carolina, where her interests include ballroom dance, bridge, needlepoint, and her dogs Cha-Cha (shown) and Panther.